15

JUNIOR

CLASSICS

Published by
Rupa Publications India Pvt. Ltd 2016
7/16, Ansari Road, Daryaganj
New Delhi 110002

Sales centres:
Bengaluru Chennai
Hyderabad Jaipur Kathmandu
Kolkata Mumbai Prayagraj

This is a work of fiction. Names, characters, places and incidents are either the product of the author's imagination or are used fictitiously and any resemblance to any actual person, living or dead, events or locales is entirely coincidental.

P-ISBN: 978-81-291-3899-6
E-ISBN: 978-81-291-4322-8

Third impression 2023

10 9 8 7 6 5 4 3

Printed in India

Contents

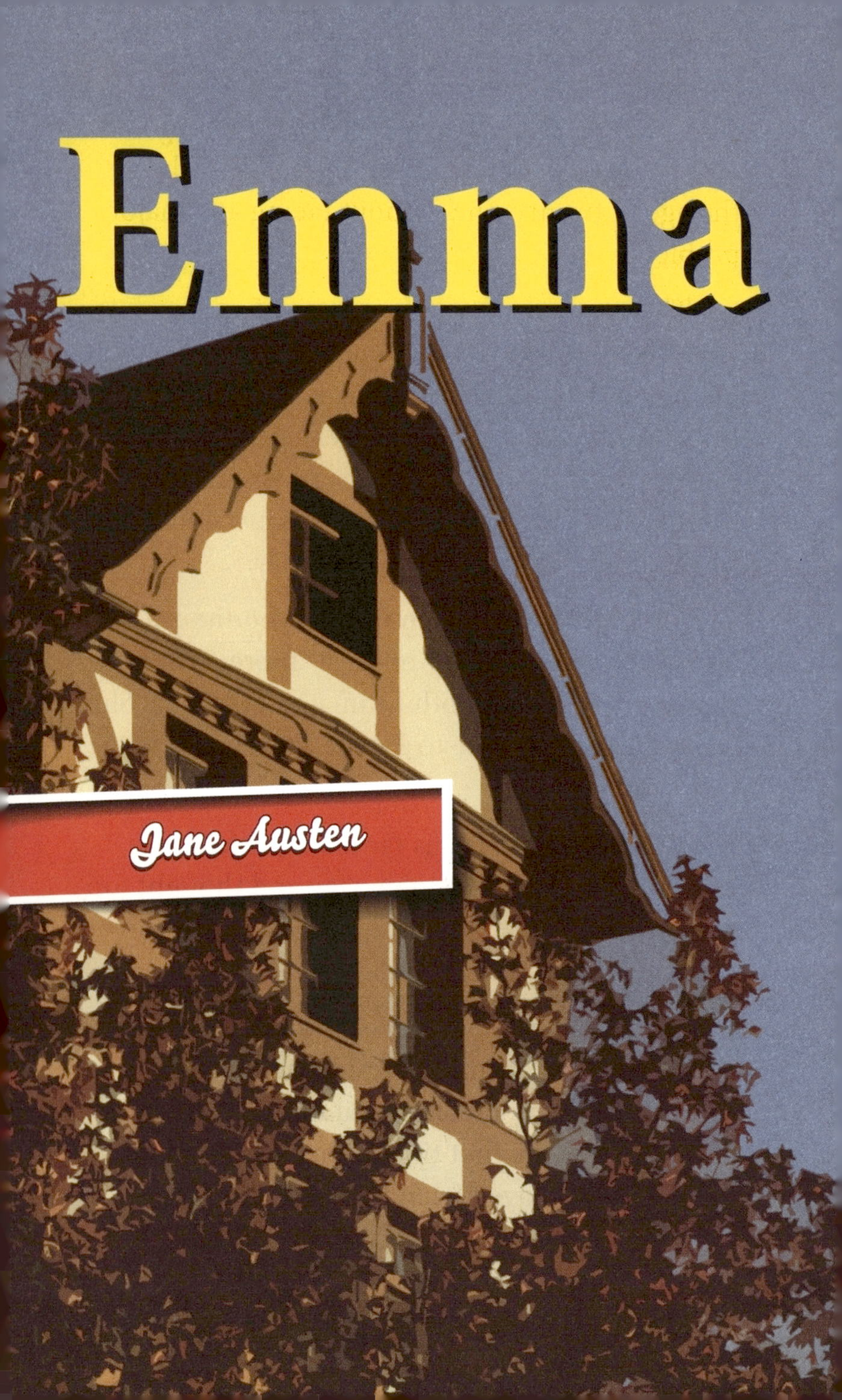
Emma
Jane Austen

Emma Woodhouse was clever, rich, good-looking and friendly, and had reached the age of twenty-one without facing any major problems.

The younger of two daughters of an easygoing and affectionate widower, she lived a comfortable life in a comfortable house. After her sister Isabella got married, Emma learned to be mistress of their home, Hartfield, at a very young age. Her mother had died when Emma was just a little girl, so she remembered her only vaguely.

Miss Taylor, had been in the Woodhouse family for sixteen years, and was more a friend than a governess to both Emma and Isabella. She was particularly close to Emma and shared with her a sisterly bond.

However, Emma was far from perfect. She was used to having her own way and thought too much about herself. These qualities were a threat to many of her life's enjoyments.

Emma felt a gentle sorrow on the day Miss Taylor married Mr Weston, who was a widower. He was a man of suitable age and good manners. For the first time in her life, Emma felt the loss of a beloved friend.

Emma missed Miss Taylor terribly, even though the new Mrs Weston did not live too far away. Emma's father may not have been very old in years, but his nature was that of an elderly man. Isabella lived in London, and although it was only sixteen miles away, Emma could not make daily trips there. Her life lit up only at Christmas time when Isabella and her family visited.

The village of Highbury, in which Hartfield was situated, did not afford her any company of equal stature since everyone looked up to the Woodhouses. Emma's father was on good terms with everyone, but he was a nervous person who disliked change of any kind. He believed that Miss Taylor should not have married, but spent all her life at Hartfield.

'I wish Miss Taylor were here!' he said one morning.

'I don't agree with you', Emma replied. 'Mr Weston is a good man who is worthy of a good wife like Miss Taylor.'

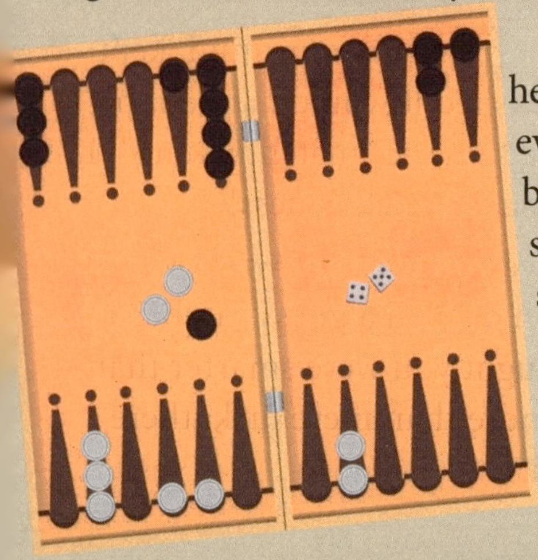

Emma hoped to get her father get through the evening with a game of backgammon. However, she did not need to, since a visitor arrived, who could play against Mr Woodhouse. Mr Knightley was an old family friend. He was also the brother of John Knightley, Isabella's husband. A sensible man in his late thirties, he lived a mile away, visited frequently and was always welcome. This time he was more than welcome, having just returned from Isabella's house in Brunswick Square, London.

Mr Woodhouse asked him many questions about 'poor Isabella' and Mr Knightley reassured him, and made him happy.

Incidentally, Mr Knightley was the only person who saw Emma's faults and pointed them out to her. Emma did not like this, and her father found it even less pleasant.

The conversation turned to the marriage of Miss Taylor and how much the Woodhouses missed her.

'Her marriage is of particular joy to me for I myself made the match,' Emma said.

But Mr Knightley said he did not think so.

'You planned the marriage in your mind, kept thinking about it and wished it would happen,' he asserted. 'That's not the same as "matchmaking"! I can only say that you made a lucky guess!'

Emma replied, 'Have you ever known how pleasurable the triumph of such a guess can be? I have pity on you. I thought you were smarter than that. A lucky guess is more than mere luck; there is some talent involved.'

Mr Woodhouse interjected and told Emma that she must not make any more matches.

'There's just one more! I must seek a wife for poor Mr Elton,' Emma said, referring to the young vicar of Highbury, who lived alone (and wished he didn't).

'Bring him to dinner here one day. I'm sure Mr Knightley would like to meet him,' Mr Woodhouse said.

Mr Knightley laughed in good manner at this suggestion and said it would give him great pleasure to come.

However, he cautioned Emma, 'Let him select his own wife. A twenty-eight-year-old man is capable of looking after himself.'

***

Mr Weston, whom Miss Taylor got married to, came from a respectable family and after gaining good breeding, some property and a good education, became independent early in life. But unlike his brothers who were engaged in homely pursuits, Mr Weston entered his country's military. Then, when Mr Weston became Captain Weston, he met Miss Churchill, who belonged to a prominent Yorkshire family. She fell in love with him, which upset her brother and his wife, but as she was of age and commanded her own fortune, she married Weston, which greatly humilated the

Churchills. Her marriage was not a happy one. She missed her luxurious life and home at Enscombe and wanted to be, at the same time, Captain Weston's wife—and Miss Churchill of Enscombe. However, three years into the marriage, and the birth of a son Frank, she died of a lingering illness.

Since Mr and Mrs Churchill had no children, they offered to take care of little Frank. And so Frank was put in the care of the Churchills and their wealth.

Weston meanwhile left the military and took up a trade with his brothers in London. He spent his leisure days in Highbury, where he still had a house. He spent the next eighteen to twenty years of his life in work and leisure, and eventually had enough money to buy Randalls, a property he had been eyeing for many years. He had made his fortune, bought his house, and obtained his wife; and was beginning a new period of existence, with every probability of being happier than ever before.

Frank Churchill was someone Highbury could boast of, though he had yet to visit that place. Now that his father had married again, it was widely believed he would make that trip.

The hope drew strength from the fact that he had written a 'handsome' letter to his new mother of which many people were talking about.

***

Mr Woodhouse liked to have friends around him in the evenings, even though he did not have much interaction with people beyond his own circle. He hated late hours and large parties, but had a few chosen friends for dinner. Among those who came to his table—including those frequenters at the evening card games—Mr Knightley, the Westons and Mr Elton comprised the first, upper set of visitors.

In the second rung, you could count Mrs Goddard, who ran a school, Miss Bates and her mother Mrs Bates. The three ladies were picked up and dropped in the Woodhouse family carriage by the driver James, who did not look upon this task as a hardship.

Miss Bates was one those ladies who were very popular because they were neither handsome nor rich, or young and unmarried. She had no intellectual superiority and was neither beautiful nor intelligent. She had not distinguished herself in her youth and had devoted her middle life to taking care of her mother and striving to make frugal ends meet. But she was a happy woman; she had everyone's goodwill, was genuinely interested in their happiness and gave merit where it was due. She felt she was a very fortunate person, blessed many times over and had so many good friends and neighbours. In sum, Miss Bates wanted for nothing.

One morning, Mrs Goddard sent Emma a note, asking her if she could bring Miss Smith along with her that evening. Emma knew the young Miss Smith and was interested in her due to the latter's good looks and returned a gracious invitation.

Harriet Smith's parents had placed her some years back at Mrs Goddard's school and later raised her condition to a parlour-boarder. They never visited, and she didn't have any known friends. She had the kind of beauty that Emma admired: regular features, plump, short and fair, blue eyes, light hair and a sweet look. Emma was determined to maintain her friendship with Harriet.

In a manner of speaking, Emma took over Harriet. She invited and encouraged her and told her to come frequently to the Woodhouses. Harriet was an even better walking companion than Mrs Weston: Emma had nothing to do for Mrs Weston; for Harriet she had everything to do.

Harrriet had spent two months at Abbey-Mill Farm with the Martins family and she had happy memory of those days which she shared with Emma. She was especially talking about the

Martins's son who was twenty-four years old and who had made her happy in several ways—like going around three miles to get Harriet the walnuts she liked so much. Harriet spoke happily about their evening games and moonlight walks and focused on his good humour and obliging nature.

Emma suspected danger lay ahead for her poor Harriet and she, Emma, must take things in her hand. She asked Harriet if she could read and the young girl said she had read *The Vicar of Wakefield*, but besides that, only farm manuals. Then Emma popped the question of Martin's looks and Harriet replied, 'He's not handsome … In fact he's quite plain.'

They happened to meet Mr Martin the next day itself, while they were out walking. Emma moved ahead to give them a chance to be together and her sharp eye took in Robert Martin. Besides seeming to be a sensible man, Martin possessed no advantage in Emma's estimation.

'Miss Woodhouse, what do you think of him? Is he very plain?' Harriet asked when she got together with Emma a few minutes later.

Emma did not mince her words, 'He is remarkably plain and he absolutely doesn't have any high social status. He is very clownish and without air.'

'He is not polite like true gentlemen,' an annoyed Harriet whispered.

'Harriet, at Hartfield, you have seen good specimens of real gentlemen.'

When Harriet mentioned Mr Knightley, Emma told her to compare Martin with Mr Weston and Mr Elton, how they talked, walked and conducted themselves in general.

'But Mr Weston is so old ...'

'A man's manner improves as he grows old,' Emma said. 'Bad manners are acceptable in one's youth but disliked in older people. Mr Martin now is abrupt and awkward. How do you imagine he would be at Mr Weston's age?'

The two ladies continued their conversation in this vein till Emma asserted, 'Young men must take the good-humoured, well-mannered and respectable Elton as their role model', and went on to sing Mr Elton's praises.

Harriet smiled as she blushed and said she found Mr Elton a very agreeable person. He was Highbury's vicar and the smallness of his vicarage was made up by a piece of independent property that he owned.

***

Mr Knightley told Mrs Weston quite plainly that he did not like the 'great intimacy' that had sprung up between Emma and Harriet.

'I feel it's a bad thing. They will not do any good to one another.'

'You amaze me! I get the greatest pleasure watching their intimacy. It's clear we feel very differently on this issue,' Mrs Weston said. 'Maybe it is a sign of our not seeing eye-to-eye on some subjects and the beginning of our quarrels!'

'You are probably thinking that I've purposely come to quarrel with you, especially since your husband is out and you can assert yourself in a better way!'

'My husband would have supported me,' replied Mrs Weston. 'You are used to living alone so much that you don't value the friendship of a companion!'

That wasn't the last word these two people had between themselves that day. They went on and on with neither of them willing to accept defeat.

***

Now Emma was confident of bringing about a match between Harriet and Mr Elton. When the latter visited one day, Emma asked Harriet if she would like to have her portrait done. Mr Elton exclaimed that it was a good idea for

Emma to use her painting skill on her friend and so Emma drew a good likeness of Harriet which was admired by the girl, and Mr Elton was enthusiastic in his praise. It took more than one sitting for the drawing to be completed and on each occasion, Mr Elton pleaded that he be called to watch the proceedings.

Mr Knightley said that Emma had made Harriet 'too tall' and Mr Elton quickly replied that wasn't so.

The picture had to be framed and, since it was December, Mr Woodhouse wouldn't dream of Emma going out in the thick fog to get the job done. Mr Elton volunteered to get the picture framed in London and Emma thought to herself, 'Mr Elton is a great man … he will suit Harriet well.'

***

The day Mr Elton went to London, Emma got more reason to help her closest friend. The extraordinary thing that happened was that Mr Martin had sent a parcel for Harriet and when it was opened it contained, among other things, a letter of a marriage proposal!

The letter's style was quite above Emma's expectation. Though the language was plain it was unaffected and strong and conveyed sentiments very much to the credit of the writer.

'You must answer it quickly,' Emma told Harriet.

'You think I should refuse him?' asked Harriet.

Emma answered, 'Of course. I thought you wanted my guidance only in the wording of your reply. However, I will not give you advice on the matter of your feelings, which you must resolve yourself.'

Thus Harriet's reply was written, sealed and dispatched. Harriet was a bit low all evening, but Emma had no feeling for Harriet's manner.

'Think of your picture, which Mr Elton has with him!'

'He has kept my portrait in Bond Street,' replied Harriet.

'Your picture won't be in Bond Street for long. It will be Mr Elton's

delight and solace. It will give his family clues to his future designs.'

Harriet's smile grew broader.

***

Since Harriet was away at Mrs Goddard's, Mr Knightley sat down for a chat with Emma. To Emma's surprise, he was full of praise for the girl. He went on to tell Emma that she had made Harriet a better person and had convinced her to stop giggling like a schoolgirl!

Mr Knightley revealed to Emma that Harriet Smith would soon get a marriage offer from Martin.

'He came to consult me on the matter two days back. He wanted to know if I approved of the match. I liked his choice completely. He is a fine young man who has some very good qualities.'

Then, smilingly, Emma told Mr Knightley that Martin had written a proposal to Harriet the day before and it had been turned down!

Mr Knightley turned red with displeasure and in anger said, 'She is a bigger simpleton than I thought! What is the foolish girl planning?'

Mr Knightley almost lost his temper as he and Emma argued about the qualities of Harriet. He told Emma that Mr Elton would only marry a girl

who had money. He said Mr Elton knew a family of several sisters who each had £20,000. The argument finally ended when the two headstrong people got upset with each other and parted ways abruptly. Harriet's return lifted Emma's spirits. She told Emma that Mr Elton was on a mission concerning a certain lady.

***

Harriet and Emma were collecting 'charades', or riddles, and pasting them in a book, when Mr Elton returned with Harriet's framed portrait. He also contributed a riddle and when Harriet could not solve it, Emma solved it and the word turned out to be 'courtship'. When she told Mr Elton this, he showed his appreciation. Emma thought that he had Harriet on his mind and it was she he was praising.

One day, Harriet and Emma visited a poor family who lived near Mr Elton's vicarage. While they were making their way there, Harriet expressed her astonishment that Emma was still unmarried. In reply, Emma explained that she had resolved to stay single. They were busy assisting the poor family but the girls' thoughts turned to Mr Elton, who they had met on the road. Emma tried to leave the two together by falling behind them. Later, she used the excuse of needing a ribbon to lace her shoes and asked Mr Elton if they could stop at his house. Mr Elton did not show any interest in Harriet, but Emma just thought he was a slow lover and was not discouraged.

***

Emma's sister, Isabella, her husband and their children arrived at Hartfield and Emma was pre-occupied with them for some time. Emma didn't like the strict manner in which John Knightley treated his wife and children. Hartfield, like Highbury, was awash in speculation on whether or not Mr Weston's son Mr Frank Churchill would visit.

Meanwhile, Mr Knightley and Emma came to a sort of resolution, although they still didn't agree about whom Harriet should marry. Mr Knightley said that Martin was extremely disappointed at being rejected by Harriet. Isabella had heard all the latest gossip at Highbury and she thought that Miss Bates's niece, Jane Fairfax, could be a good friend for Emma. Isabella's husband decided that he and his family would visit a beach resort that autumn and not come to Hartfield as they usually did.

The Knightleys and the Woodhouses accepted an invitation to spend Christmas Eve at the Westons. Though Mr Elton and Harriet were also invited, a sore throat forced her to skip the gathering. Emma was surprised when Mr Elton refused to stay back with Harriet.

Mr John Knightley, who witnessed the conversation, felt that Mr Elton's feelings were for Emma—a suggestion which an amused Emma summarily dismissed. Emma travelled to the dinner in the same carriage as Mr Elton. She was astonished at his cheerfulness, as she had expected him to be quite upset since Harriet was ill.

Mr Elton's strange behaviour continued all through the party. He stayed beside her all evening, and eventually, Emma had to admit that her brother-in-law may have been right: Mr Elton was in love with her. When Mr Weston announced that Frank Churchill would be visiting in January, Emma felt a stirring in her for she had once thought of Frank as her likely suitor.

Suddenly, it began to snow heavily. Everyone wondered how they would make it back safely. Eventually, Emma found herself in the same carriage as Mr Elton, who asked her to marry him. She turned him down, and he got angry when she explained about Harriet. He did not think Harriet was suited to his social station.

***

As she continued towards Hartfield, Emma thought about the issue over in her head. Her biggest disappointment was that Harriet's feelings for Mr Elton were largely fuelled by her own encouragement. She also recognized that the Knightley brothers had been correct about Elton. Emma vowed to renounce matchmaking; she couldn't help coming up with possible suitors for Harriet, but kept reminding herself of her previous failure.

Mr and Mrs Knightley returned to London and Mr Elton went off on a holiday to Bath, much to the relief of Emma, who now wondered if the sweet Harriet was not a 'more superior person' than her. Emma also got Harriet ready for Mr Elton's inevitable return to Highbury.

January came and went, but Frank Churchill did not visit, since his aunt was very ill. Mrs Weston was naturally disappointed. Emma had other worries; but, around Mrs Weston, she behaved normally with regard to Frank. This upset Mr Knightley. Emma said that when Frank did actually come to Highbury, he would be charming to have around. But Mr Knightley believed he would be insufferable and superficial. Emma was stunned by Mr Knightley's judgement of a man he had not even met!

***

One morning, Emma was walking with Harriet, when she decided she had heard enough about Mr Elton. She tried to turn Harriet's thoughts away from Mr Elton, but with little success. Therefore, she suggested a visit to the Bates's home, something she normally did not like doing. Once there, Emma was forced to listen to how famously Mr Elton was getting along with the society at Bath. Then, she also had to hear about a letter from Jane Fairfax, Miss Bates's niece, who lived with her guardians, a Colonel and Mrs Campbell. Jane would be arriving at Highbury for an extended visit, since the Campbells were preparing to visit their newly married daughter, Mrs Dixon, in Ireland. When Emma heard that Mr Dixon had once saved Jane when she fell off a boat, and that he was very attentive to her, she jumped to the conclusion that Jane had been romantically involved with Mr Dixon before his marriage. This, she assumed, was why Jane Fairfax was not going to visit her friend, Mrs Dixon, in Ireland.

Miss Bates was not aware of Emma's reasoning, and continued talking about Jane.

She said Jane's father had died in battle when she was just three. Her mother, Mrs Bates's youngest daughter, wasted away soon after from grief and consumption, and Jane moved to Highbury. When she was eight, Colonel Campbell—who had been her father's friend—took her in. He could not give her an inheritance, but would pay for Jane's education—a move that would ensure her employment as a governess when she got old enough.

By and by, Jane arrived in Highbury after a two-year absence. She had apparently met Frank Churchill along the way, but Emma could get no information about what kind of man he was, or any details on their friendship. Emma was vaguely irritated by Jane's presence, but did not understand why. She was shocked at Mr Knightley suggestion that she was simply jealous of the younger girl.

Mr Knightley said he had something to tell Emma, but was interrupted by the sudden arrival of the Bates. They beat Mr Knightley in telling Emma that Mr Elton had got engaged to a Miss Hawkins. Just then, Harriet rushed in to tell them that she met Mr Martin and his sister in town. They had greeted her very kindly, she said. But Emma distracted her by telling her about Mr Elton's forthcoming marriage.

Miss Hawkins caused a stir in Highbury—she was accomplished, beautiful and had a tidy fortune. Harriet was quite upset at the thought of the impending wedding, and Emma could only distract her by talking about the Martins.

A few days later, Martin's sister Elizabeth left a note for Harriet at Mrs Goddard's, asking her to visit them.

Emma and Harriet discussed the matter, and decided that Emma would go with Harriet, leave and then return to pick her up in fifteen minutes. Harriet spent the time with Mrs Martin and Elizabeth, who were quite insulted when Emma returned so soon. They understood that Emma was ashamed to have Harriet spend time with 'inferior' people like the Martins.

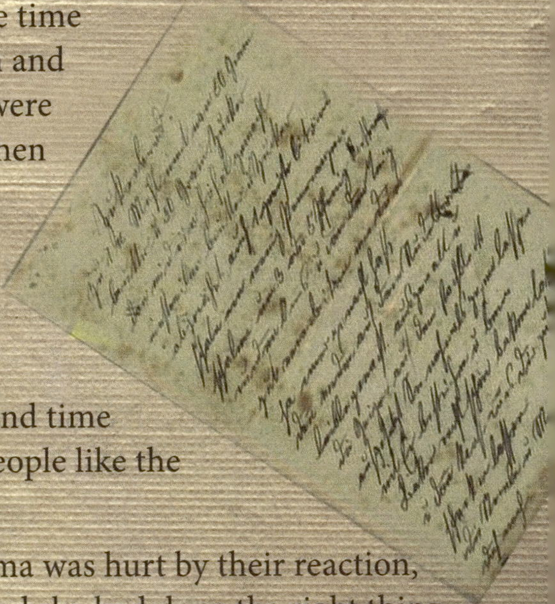

Though Emma was hurt by their reaction, she was convinced she had done the right thing.

Emma's spirits were soon lifted. Frank Churchill had arrived at Hartfield. She was impressed with his good looks, intelligence and charm. As they talked, he told Emma he thought Jane was plain and unattractive.

However, Emma's good impression of Frank Churchill was dented when he made a trip to London merely to have a haircut. Mr Knightley continued to think of Frank as a silly fellow.

Meanwhile, the Coles, a family of successful tradespersons, were having a party. Emma did not want to be associated with them, but when the Woodhouses did not receive an invitation, Emma felt left out. So, when the invitation finally arrived, she decided to accept it.

At the party, Emma discovered that Jane had received a piano as a gift from a mysterious sender. Emma at once decided it was from Mr Dixon; everyone else thought it was from Colonel Campbell. Jane just blushed and refused to say anything on the subject.

Emma noticed that Mr Knightley came to the party in his

carriage, instead of walking as he normally did. She mentioned this to Mrs Weston, who said he had brought it, so he could drive Emma home. She also suggested that Mr Knightley was beginning to have feelings for Emma. Emma vigorously argued against this idea, saying that Mr Knightley's marriage would mean her nephew Henry—George and Isabella's son—would not inherit the Knightleys' estate of Donwell Abbey.

Throughout the party, Frank ignored Jane and paid special attention to Emma, who imagined that he would eventually ask her to marry him and be turned down. As much as Emma liked him, she did not think she loved him enough to marry him.

***

When Mr Elton came to Highbury with his bride, Emma and Harriet were the first to welcome the new couple. Emma reserved her opinion on Mrs Elton. When Mr and Mrs Elton paid a return visit to Hartfield, Emma watched Mrs Elton at great length and formed her opinion about her. She didn't like her manners which she felt were 'too familiar'. She also disliked her attachment to superficial symbols of wealth like a '*barouche-landau*'—a French carriage that belonged to her sister and brother-in-law.

***

Mrs Elton noted that Emma disliked her, and returned the feeling. The Eltons were particularly rude to Harriet, and Emma thought that Mr Elton had told his wife about the regrettable incident that resulted from her matchmaking.

Jane responded favourably to Mrs Elton's attempts to involve her in the social scene. She also declined another invite to join the Campbells and Dixons in Ireland, leaving Emma puzzled.

When Mr Knightley said he approved of Jane accepting Mrs Elton's attention, Emma probed him about his feelings for Miss Fairfax. She pointed out the coincidence of him arriving in a carriage the day the piano was delivered, and said Miss Bates had mentioned how he had sent the last of his orchard's apples to Jane Fairfax.

'Everyone knows how highly I think of her,' he said.

To which Emma replied, 'Perhaps, even you may not know the extent of your affection! The extent of your admiration may take you by surprise some day.'

A disturbed Mr Knightley wondered if Emma was playing matchmaker for him! When she told

him she was not, he insisted that he didn't love Jane—and Emma found herself oddly content.

***

The next time Emma met Frank, he behaved in a spirited and friendly way but stayed for just fifteen minutes. This brief visit convinced Emma that Frank's feelings for her had weakened. Meanwhile, Mrs Churchill finally decided that the Churchill family would shift from London to Richmond, which meant that Frank would be closer to Highbury. Mr Weston was thrilled that his son would be nearer to him and plans for a ball—postponed indefinitely when Frank returned to his aunt's house—were revived.

Before Frank had left, he had started to tell her something that appeared to be a secret, but was interrupted. Now, Emma wanted to ask him about it, and was happy when Mr Weston called her early to oversee the arrangements for the ball. However, Mr Weston had called others early too, and Frank was very fidgety, as if he was expecting someone. When Miss Bates and Jane arrived, he sprang forward to assist them with their umbrellas. Frank then rushed to his father to ask when the dancing would begin.

The Westons realized that Mrs Elton wanted to lead the dancing, and so they could not give that honour to Emma. Nevertheless Emma enjoyed the ball.

At one point, Harriet was without a dance partner, and Mr Elton refused to ask her to dance, even though he also had no partner. Mr Knightley—who had not danced till then—watched Emma keenly and asked Harriet to dance, thus sparing her embarrassment. This pleased Emma no end. She thanked Mr Knightley for his gesture to Harriet and when he asked her why the Eltons were her enemies, she said because she had wanted Mr Elton to marry Harriet. Emma and Mr Knightley then celebrated their new-found understanding by dancing with each other.

In the meantime, Harriet and her friend had gone for a walk and become surrounded by gypsies, who demanded money from them. Luckily, Frank was nearby and scared off the gypsies.

***

Harriet now confided in Emma that she was no longer fascinated by Mr Elton, and threw the trinkets she had kept in memory of him, into the fire. She went on to say she would never marry. Recalling how Frank had rescued Harriet earlier that evening, Emma thought he might replace Mr Elton in Harriet's affections. She asked if Harriet

had feelings for someone above her rank. When Harriet said yes, Emma—who assumed she meant Frank—advised her to be cautious, but to not lose hope. What Emma did not know was that Harriet had started to look favourably on Mr Knightley!

A few days later, Emma, Harriet, Mr and Mrs Weston, Frank, Jane, and Miss Bates and Mr Knightley were taking a walk together. Frank asked Mrs Weston about someone buying a carriage. Mrs Weston asked how he knew about that, and he said she had mentioned it in a letter. However, Mrs Weston was quite sure she had not. She later remembered that her husband had talked about it, when Jane was present. Realizing that there was a secret connection between Frank and Jane, Mr Knightley warned Emma, but she laughed at him, and said she knew why Frank did not like Jane. Her attitude irritated Mr Knightley, but he did not show his irritation.

Later, the group took a trip to Donwell Abbey, where Emma enjoyed examining Mr Knightley's house and grounds. She also overheard Mrs Elton try to force Jane to accept a job as a governess. Jane refused to make a decision until the Campbells returned from their trip.

The next day, the group went on a picnic to Box Hill, but it was a failure. The Eltons didn't mingle with the others while Mr Knightley, Jane and Miss Bates formed their own exclusive group. Emma remained with Frank and Harriet. Frank tried to enliven the outing and asked each member of the group to do one thing exceedingly clever, or two slightly clever or three dull things! Miss Bates humorously said she could easily do the last requirement. In reply to this, Emma replied that she would only be allowed three dull things. Her jovial attitude confused Miss Bates at first, but she soon realized that she had been insulted, and grew red in embarrassment. Mr Weston made up a puzzle, in praise of Emma, and the Eltons left the party to take a walk. Mrs Elton had said that she was disgusted by such activities.

Later, Mr Knightley scolded Emma for her behaviour.

'How could you be so harsh to Miss Bates? How could you be so insolent in your wit to a woman of her character, age, and situation?' he said. 'And don't tell me she misunderstood you. She understood perfectly. I just wish you had heard her talk of the event; heard her honouring your patience in paying attention to her, when you obviously found her annoying.'

'I know there is not a better creature in the world, but you cannot deny that she is a mixture of both the good and the ridiculous!' Emma replied.

'I know that but remember that she has had an unfortunate life. She has lost her comforts in life and become poor; remember that she will probably lose even more as she becomes older. She deserves your compassion, not your scorn!' Knightley said, and then walked away.

Emma was ashamed, and decided to visit the Bates the next morning to apologize.

Emma returned from the Bates to find Mr Knightley and Harriet sitting with her father at Hartfield. When Mr Woodhouse asked Emma about her visit to the Bates, Emma looked at Mr Knightley quickly, and from his look, guessed that he understood her, and forgave her. As he was leaving, Mr Knightley—who said he had come to say goodbye to her as he was leaving for a visit to his brother's house in London—took Emma's

hand and almost kissed it. Emma was pleased but puzzled as to why he did not complete the kiss.

The next day, they received news that Mrs Churchill had died. For a while, Emma thought this would make it easier for Harriet and Frank to get married. Then, she visited Randalls, and Mrs Weston told her that Frank had quietly got engaged to Jane. Mrs Weston was worried about Emma, since Frank had been flirting with her all the time. Emma reassured Mrs Weston that she had no affection for Frank. However, she added that she was upset with Frank for behaving rudely towards Jane.

Most of all, Emma was embarrassed about the things she had told Frank about Jane, and about Harriet's feelings. However, it turned out that Harriet was never interested in Frank. When she had admitted to having feelings for someone above her rank, she had been talking of Mr Knightley!

At this point, Emma realized she did not want Mr Knightley to marry anyone else. To her own surprise, she had fallen in love with him! Without revealing her own feelings, she asked Harriet if she thought Mr Knightley paid special attention to Emma. Harriet had to agree.

Emma was walking in the garden, when Mr Knightley—just back from London—joined her. He had heard about Frank and Jane's engagement. He thought Emma would be unhappy about it, and expressed his regret. However, once Emma confessed that she had no feelings for Frank, Mr Knightley exclaimed that he loved her. Emma was thrilled! Within half an hour Mr Knightley and Emma had become engaged.

That night, Emma lay in bed worrying about Harriet and her father. She decided to write Harriet a letter explaining everything, and make arrangements for Harriet to go to Isabella's house in London, to give them time to adjust to the new circumstances. Since she did not want to leave her father alone at Hartfield, she also decided that she and her new fiancé could not get married until her father died.

Mrs Weston then sent a letter to Emma that Frank wrote, in which he explained that his special treatment to Emma was because he wanted to hide his engagement to Jane. Emma showed the letter to Mr Knightley. Although he was less inclined to forgive Frank, Mr Knightley admitted that Frank was not really a bad chap. Above all, Mr Knightley said the two of them could live at Hartfield, with Mr Woodhouse, after the wedding—which pleased Emma no end.

There was more good news in store: Robert Martin had proposed to Harriet again, and she had accepted.

All three couples were married before the year ended: Mr Martin and Harriet in September, Emma and Mr Knightley in October and Jane and Frank in November.

Jane Eyre
Charlotte Brontë

The afternoon was chilly and there was no chance of taking a walk. I was sad because nurse Bessie had scolded me, and I was aware that I was not as physically strong as my cousins John, Georgiana and Eliza Reed. The three of them were gathered around their mama, as she rested in the drawing room near a fireside in the house at Gateshead. I was kept out of the group, until Bessie gave her 'report' about me and Mrs Reed herself formed her own opinion about me. I was told to keep quiet and sit somewhere.

I began reading my book again. It was *Bewick's History of British Birds*, and it gave me great pleasure though I was only ten years old. However, I was soon interrupted.

It was John Reed and he shouted, 'Madame Mope! Where is she? Georgy! Lizzy! Where is that bad animal?'

I thought to myself, 'It's good that I had drawn the curtain'.

But Eliza gave me away. 'John, surely, she is on the window seat.'

I left my nook and asked John what he wanted.

'Address me as Master Reed,' the boy answered. 'Come here.'

John was fourteen years old, stout and large. He had dim eyes and flabby cheeks. His mother had removed him from school due to 'delicate

health'. The schoolmaster, Mr Miles, had said the boy should be eating less sweets but his mother opined that the lad was simply homesick.

John punished and bullied me continually, and there was nothing I could do about it. Mrs Reed turned a blind eye to his taunts, and the servants were not keen to back me since they were scared of annoying their master.

John hit me hard, and said, 'You rat, that was for being impudent to my mother and for hiding behind the curtains!'

'Let me see the book you were reading behind the curtain,' he said.

I gave it to him, and he flung it at me. It hit me, and I fell, striking my head against the door and cutting it. The cut bled, and the pain was sharp but I was now more angry than terrified.

'You cruel, wicked boy … you are just like the Roman rulers—a murderer!' I shouted.

John ran into me headlong and held my shoulder and hair. He called me, 'Rat!' and bellowed loudly.

Soon, Georgiana and Eliza rushed to fetch Mrs Reed. Bessie followed them along with Abbot and four hands caught me tight.

'Lock her in the red room,' said Mrs Reed, and I was taken upstairs to that chamber.

The red room was a very stately chamber with a huge bed in the middle and two large windows. The windows were always closed, and the room was not generally used, since this was where my uncle, Mr Reed, died nine years ago.

Bessie and Abbot wanted to tie me up but relented when I promised to sit still.

Bessie warned me, 'Remember, Miss, you are obliged to Mrs Reed. She looks after you; if she turns you out, you'll end up in the poorhouse.'

This reminder of my dependence was nothing new to me—they had drummed it into my head.

'And you are not an equal of Master Reed and Misses Reed just because Missis is kindly bringing you up,' they added for good measure.

I asked myself, 'Why was I the one to suffer all this? Why was I always bullied, bruised and humiliated?'

I was the noisy note in Gateshead Hall.

Suddenly I heard noises and a ghostly voice—the ghost of my dear uncle who had died here. I screamed in fright and the maids came rushing in to ask what the matter was.

'Are you unwell, Miss Eyre?' asked Bessie.

'What a terrible noise!' said Abbot.

I cried out, 'Take me to the nursery!'

'Are you injured?' asked Bessie.

'Oh! I imagined a ghost was entering the room!' I said as I gripped Bessie's hand.

'Forgive me! Punish me in another way!' I said to my aunt when she entered the room.

'Quiet! All this violence is ugly.'

In her eyes I was a gifted actress and she looked down on me as a combination of dangerous passions, bad spirit and dangerous duplicity.

Mrs Reed pushed me back in and locked me up. As she left, I had some kind of fit and fell down unconscious.

I had a horrific nightmare in which I saw a dreadful red glare before me that was crossed with broad black bars. I also heard voices and an all-pervading sense of fear gripped me. When I awoke, I was resting in my own bed and the red glare was the fire in the nursery.

Bessie treated me very kindly and a gentleman sat beside me on a chair by my bed. He was Mr Lloyd, the doctor.

'Do you know who I am?' he asked.

I said his name and offered him my hand.

'You'll be well soon,' he assured me.

When Dr Lloyd returned in the morning, he asked me, 'Your name is Jane?'

I answered, 'Yes, Jane Eyre.'

'What happened to you?' he asked, and Bessie helped me explain to him that I had seen a ghost.

As the conversation became more personal, he asked me, 'Do you not like staying at Gateshead Hall?'

'No,' I replied. 'I am an orphan. I have been treated badly here by my cousin John and my aunt.'

'Do you have any relations?

'I think so … Aunt Reed once told me about a certain Eyre family … but she did not know much about them. They are poor and I would not like to live with a poor family.'

'Do you want to go to school?'

I thought long on this question and finally replied, 'I certainly want to go to school.'

Later, Bessie entered the room and I learned, for the first time (from information that Abbot gave to Bessie) that my father had died of typhus, contracted while serving the poor as a clergyman and that—because my mother had married him against the wishes of her family—she had been cut off without a penny. She had died after catching the typhus from her husband.

After I regained my health, Mrs Reed rarely spoke to me. She kept me apart from her own children and made me sleep in a small closet. I was condemned to eat alone, and stay in the nursery all the while. Not a word was said about my schooling.

Eliza, Georgiana and John kept insulting me and fury and revolt again stirred in my bosom, but I refrained from doing anything about it.

Christmas came and went, and then New Year, but I was left out of all the festivities. My share of the celebrations lay in watching Georgiana and Eliza dressing up, and then listening to the music being played below. I had a doll, which was my best friend. I carried her with me everywhere and she snuggled with me in bed.

On January 15, a man in a carriage came to the house and I was called by my aunt.

The visitor's prying eyes twinkled below his bushy eye-brows.

'She is small; what's her age?' he asked in a bass and solemn voice.

'Ten,' my aunt said. 'Mr Brocklehurst, let's not talk about that anymore.'

The next day, on a chilly winter morning, I left Gateshead for school. Bessie saw me off and hugged me tightly. I don't remember much of the journey except that it seemed to cover hundreds of miles.

I reached the school at last and was greeted by a tall woman who had an erect bearing.

'Miss Miller,' she said to her companion, 'she seems to be tired and hungry. Give her some food.'

The tall woman asked me some personal questions.

'I hope she will be a good girl,' she told Miss Miller as she dismissed us.

Miss Miller escorted me through passage after passage, in the huge, irregular-shaped building. I heard the murmur of students studying before we reached a long wide room where there were many tables.

I saw what looked like hundreds of children of all ages—although, in reality, they were only about eighty—seated there, dressed in the school uniform.

We were given our meals after which Miss Miller read the prayers. The children filed off to their beds in twos. I was so tired that I quickly fell asleep.

All the girls cursed the 'burnt porridge' the next morning, even the four teachers who were served a cup of tea but I was terribly hungry, I just couldn't put down the terrible porridge. Prayers were said and there was a reading from the Bible that lasted for an hour.

Later in the day, Miss Maria Temple, the superintendent of the school gave us a class on geography. Children of the lower classes were instructed in reading, writing and arithmetic by other teachers. Then, to our delight, she said we would be given cheese and bread—to compensate for the terrible breakfast.

Later, we were taken to the garden which was surrounded by very high walls. Since it was January, there were no flowers and the place had a decayed wintry look.

As the girls ran around playing games, I constantly heard the noise of a hollow cough.

I read the name of the institution on the gate: Lowood Institution, it said and added that it was built by Naomi Brocklehurst in a certain year. This was followed by a quotation from the Bible.

I was wondering why the place was called an 'institution' when again I heard the sound of coughing. I looked around and saw a girl sitting on a bench, reading a book strangely named *Rasselas*.

I asked her, 'Why is this place called "Institution"?'

She replied, 'Because it's a kind of charity school. You must be an orphan; are your father and mother dead?'

She carried on, 'This place is run by Mr Brocklehurst, the son of the founder Naomi. He's the manager and treasurer of the place. He belongs to the clergy and is said to do lots of good deeds.'

I learned from the girl, whose name was Helen, that of all the teachers at the school, Miss Templeton, the headmistress who had greeted me when I arrived, was the best.

'Be careful of Miss Scatcherd, don't annoy her,' Helen advised me and then told me that she had been at the school for two years.

'My mother's dead,' she added.

The bell rang for supper—and the food smelt and tasted terrible! As I ate, I wondered if the food would be like this every day.

In the afternoon, Miss Scatcherd made Helen stand alone at the middle of the large classroom as a punishment.

At five o' clock in the evening we ate another meal, then there was a half-hour of recreation and, after study, a piece of cake, water, prayers and off to bed. This, then, was my first day at the school.

The next day, I officially enrolled in the fourth class. From a spectator, I had become a participant in the institution's activities.

Miss Scatcherd continued to pick on Helen, whose last name was Burns. When it came to answering questions, particularly in history, Helen Burns seemed to know all the answers. But this did not placate Miss Scatcherd, who would suddenly pounce on the girl—'You didn't clean your nails today, you dirty girl!'

I wondered why Helen did not say that she could neither wash nor clean her nails since the water was frozen in the morning.

A few days later, I had a chance to talk to the girl. I asked her if she ever wished to escape from Lowood.

'Why should I? I was sent here to be educated. I have to attain that objective.'

'But Miss Scatcherd treats you so cruelly!'

'She's not cruel. She just doesn't like my faults. It's better to face than to retaliate; the Bible teaches us to return evil with good.'

It had been about three weeks since I came to Lowood, when Mr Brocklehurst came to visit us.

He wore a buttoned up greatcoat and looked taller, narrower and stiffer than ever. I was dismayed, for I remembered Mr Brocklehurst's promise to Mrs Reed, that he would inform my teachers of my 'vicious nature'.

However, he was too busy criticizing Miss Temple for feeding us bread and cheese. Miss Temple tried to explain that the food was awful and we could not be kept hungry all day.

But he replied, 'Madam, I want to make these girls tough, self-denying and patient.'

He then quoted from the Bible, 'If you suffer thirst or hunger for my sake, you are happy', and added, 'Miss Temple, when you feed them cheese and bread, you are feeding their degraded bodies and starving their immortal souls!'

Mr Brocklehurst paused and suddenly turned on a tall girl who had curly hair. When Miss Temple said that

the girl's hair curled naturally, Mr Brocklehurst ordered that it had to go. 'I will send a barber tomorrow!' he said, and proceeded to inspect all the girls' hair to decided who would immediately get a haircut.

Three ladies then entered the room—all of them sporting lovely curled hair. They were Mrs Brocklehurst and her two daughters.

It was my turn next. Mr Brocklehurst made me stand on a stool and told the gathering, 'The Evil One has found a place in this girl! Guard against her; reject her company, don't include her in your sports; don't talk to her. Teachers, watch her every move!'

The Brocklehursts then got up as one and sailed out of the room!

***

After I recovered from the horrible experience, Helen calmed me and told me how nobody liked Mr Brocklehurst.

Miss Temple then took us to her room.

'Have you cried away all your sorrows?' Miss Temple asked me.

I said, 'No. I will never be able to do so.'

Miss Temple then asked me about my past, 'Jane, an accused criminal is always allowed

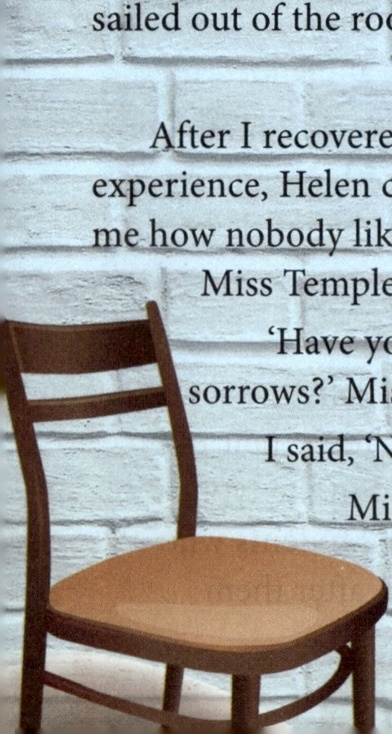

to defend himself. You've been wrongly charged, so defend yourself.'

So I told Miss Temple about the ill-treatment I received at the hands of the Reeds. When I was finished, she decided to write to Mr Lloyd to verify my story.

She then proceeded to give us a treat—tea served in china cups and toast! She told the servant Barbara to bring some bread and butter. She also asked for some seed-cake. Helen and I were given a feast!

A week later, Miss Temple received a reply from Mr Lloyd, who verified my story. Miss Temple then assembled the entire school and said that an inquiry had found that the charges against me had been entirely false!

All the teachers shook my hands and kissed me, and my school companions applauded me.

After this load was lifted from my shoulders I became a new person. I worked hard and was promoted. I was even allowed to begin classes in drawing and French.

***

The harsh conditions—especially the semi-starvation and lack of hygiene—took their toll on the girls, many of whom died in the typhus epidemic that struck the school. Students who had relatives and friends to look after them

packed up and left; the others had to stay back and risk death.

I, and other fortunate ones, however, continued to enjoy our life in the warm season and since there were fewer mouths to feed, there was ample food for the able-bodied to feed on.

But sadness again brought me down to earth, Helen fell ill.

The nurse told me, 'She won't last long,' and added, 'she's in Miss Temple's room, but you can't see her.'

That night I took a chance and crept through the school to see Helen. I found Miss Temple's room and Helen, who was awake.

'Is that you, Jane?' Helen asked.

I kissed her cold forehead. Her entire body was weak and thin.

'You are probably just in time to see me,' Helen said, 'I am at last going to my last home... I am going to God, who is good, who is my father...'

I hugged Helen tight as she breathed her last.

***

The epidemic showed up all the institution's faults—the inferior food, the dirty water used in its cooking, and the students' poor accommodation and clothing—causing Mr Brockhurst great embarrassment. However, the institution benefitted tremendously. Wealthy and generous patrons decided to build a better building in a better location; new regulations came into being; the students' clothing and diet improved greatly; and school funds were entrusted to a management committee. Because of his wealth and connections, Mr Brocklehurst retained the treasurer's post but his work was checked. The school thus became a useful and decent institution. I remained there for eight more years—six as a student and two as a teacher.

Miss Temple got married and left the school. One day, on an idea given by a friend, I advertised for the post of a tutor in *The Herald* and signed it as JE. I was just eighteen years old then.

A few days later, I walked to the town's post office and enquired if there was a letter for me.

There was indeed, and I quickly took it and raced back to the school!

This document read:

'If J.E., who advertised in the ---shire Herald of last Thursday, possesses the acquirements mentioned, and if she is in a position to give satisfactory references as to character and competency, a situation can be offered her where there is but one pupil, a little girl, under ten years of age; and where the salary is thirty pounds per annum. J.E. is requested to send references, name, address, and all particulars to the direction:—

Mrs. Fairfax, Thornfield, near Millcote, —shire.'

I was preparing to start my new life as a tutor when I got an unexpected guest—Bessie. She looked matronly yet young, and had a child with her.

I embraced her as I cried out, 'Bessie! Bessie!'

After we had settled in the parlour, she updated me on the world I had left behind so many years ago.

'That is my son,' she pointed to a small boy who was in the parlour. 'I have a daughter too. I married Leaven, the carriage driver.'

She told me that Georgiana had grown up to be a handsome woman and had almost eloped with a lord in London. They were caught 'probably by her sister, with whom she never got on well,' Bessie explained.

'John Reed was expelled from college and though his uncles are doing their best, they won't make anything much of him, I feel.'

'Mrs Reed looks well enough physically, but mentally isn't quite present,' Bessie concluded.

Then, Bessie said something that interested me specifically.

'Seven years back, a gentleman named Mr Eyre came asking about you. Missis said you were at school and he seemed quite disappointed. He said he was in a hurry as he was going to a foreign country. I think he was your father's brother.'

'What country?' I asked. 'Madeira?'

'Yes,' said Bessie.

***

I then started the next chapter of my life. A carriage was waiting at the inn at Millcote to escort me to Thornfield. Mrs Fairfax was a far better person than I had imagined. She treated me to some tea and sandwiches, and showed me to my room in a very gentle womanly manner.

When I enquired about Miss Fairfax, who I assumed would be my student, she replied, 'It's Miss Adèle Varens who is your pupil. I don't have a family.'

I politely did not make any further inquiries in the matter. Later she revealed to me that the owner of Thornfield was a certain Mr Rochester.

'I am only the housekeeper,' she explained.

'Your pupil is Mr Rochester's ward. He told me to get a governess for her.'

As I was thinking over on this, a little girl came in the lawn, followed by an attendant. She was Adèle, my pupil—seven or eight years old and small but with lots of curly hair falling to her waist.

She spoke in French and Mrs Fairfax explained that she was born on the Continent.

***

Life at Thornfield was pleasant and Adèle was a bright and exuberant child, if a bit spoiled.

One day, I was watching the moon come up while taking a walk when I saw a horse and rider on the ice. A dog was running with them. The horse suddenly reared up and slipped, and the man fell onto the ice. I rushed to help. As I introduced myself to him, the man looked at me somewhat sternly. He had a dark face and a thick brow. He was a little away from being middle-aged. When I returned to the house, the dog I had seen outside was now settled down on a rug. Mrs Fairfax then told me that the man I had met was Mr Rochester himself. He had sprained his ankle from the fall.

The next day, Mr Rochester invited me and Adèle to his room to take tea with him. He apologized for his rather rough behaviour the day before.

Mrs Fairfax later explained, 'He has had a sad personal history, that's why he sometimes behaves in this manner. His father left all the property to Mr Rochester's brother and Mr Rochester only came into it nine years back.'

I saw very little of Mr Rochester in the following days but one evening he invited Adèle and me. He was in his good, 'after dinner' moods. He gave Adèle a gift he had promised her and began to chat with me. Suddenly, he asked me, 'Do I look handsome?' and when I answered 'No' he turned cruel and started shouting at me. I put that down to his having drunk too much alcohol.

He told me, 'You are not my servant; I look upon you as an equal.'

When the conversation shifted towards the identity of Adèle's parents, he said he would explain later.

That 'later' came soon after.

He said, 'Adèle's mother was a famous dancer named Celine Varens. I was in a relationship with her, but broke it off when I found out that she was in love with another man. Adèle is not my daughter—you can see that she has none of my features.'

That night, I was lying in bed, when I suddenly smelt something burning. I ran upstairs and found the door to Mr Rochester's room open. Tongues of flame darted round the bed, the curtains were on fire. In the midst of blaze and vapour, Mr Rochester continued to sleep.

I tried to shake him awake, but by then even the sheets had caught fire. I rushed to his washstand and found two basins of water. I poured them onto the bed and its occupant. The flames were quickly moving towards him. So I rushed back to my room, got more water and quickly poured it onto him and the bed. Luckily, the fire went out. Mr Rochester awoke at last, and was confused by his bed being soaking wet.

'Is there a flood?' he cried.

'No, sir,' I answered, 'but was a fire, but I have put it out. Do get up; I will fetch you a candle.'

When I came back, Mr Rochester had changed into dry clothes, and was surveying the damage.

He was very grateful for what I had done, but told me not to reveal this incident to anybody.

***

One day, I received the terrible news that my cousin John Reed, the one who used to torture me the most, had killed himself. I rushed to Gateshead for my aunt Reed. She was in bad shape: she had suffered a stroke and had very little chance of surviving. My aunt handed me a letter which she had kept with her for three years. It read, 'I, John Eyre, wish to adopt Jane Eyre and bequeath her my fortune.' Despite my aunt's hatred—and jealousy—towards me, I did not harbour any ill will.

'Aunt,' I told her, 'I wish to be your dear friend', but my aunt did not want anything to do with me and, a few days later, she passed away.

I returned to Thornfield and one evening found myself sitting with Mr Rochester in the garden, after he had invited me there. There had been rumours that Mr Rochester planned on getting married so I was fully expecting him to tell me it was time to look for another job. However, by now, I had realized that I loved him, and did not like the idea of moving far away from Thornfield. Still, nothing prepared me for what he said.

'Jane,' Mr Rochester said, 'I sometimes have a queer feeling with regard to you—especially when you are near me. It is as if I have a string somewhere under my left ribs, tightly knotted to a similar string situated in your body. And I am afraid that, if you moved away, that cord will snap, and I would be heartbroken. As for you—you'd forget me.'

I was speechless!

Eventually, I regained my composure, and said, 'I love Thornfield—I love it because it has given me a delightful life. I am not bullied, or terrified; I have talked, face to face, with what I enjoy—with an original, a vigorous, an expanded mind. And I have met you, Mr Rochester; and it terrifies me to think that I might never see you again.

'But why do you have to leave?' he asked.

'Because you are getting married,' I replied.

'But Jane,' he said, 'it is you only I intend to marry! Jane, will you marry me?'

I said I did not believe him.

'Do you truly love me? Do you sincerely wish me to be your wife?'

He replied, 'I love you—and poor and obscure, and small and plain as you are—please say you will marry me!'

So I did.

I wanted to put myself on an equal footing with Mr Rochester after the wedding. So, I decided to write to my uncle in Madeira, asking him to include me in the Eyre family inheritance.

***

A few nights before the wedding, I awoke to a bright light in my room. I thought I had overslept, but realized it was only a candle on the nightstand. I had hung my wedding dress and veil in my closet before going to bed, but it was now open. I heard a rustling sound. I thought it was the maid, and so called out to her. When she did not respond, I got out of bed and crept towards the closet. I found that the intruder was a tall and large woman, with thick and dark hair hanging long down her back and a savage face. This strange woman picked up my veil, put it on her head, then took it off and tore into two. Then, she picked up the candle and came towards me. She held the candle under my face, and then blew it out. I was terrified, and fainted.

The next day, I told Mr Rochester about her. He convinced me that my anxious mind (I had been having nightmares) must have played a trick on me, and said he would solve the 'mystery' when we had been 'married for a year and a day'.

***

The day of my wedding arrived. On my way to the church, I saw two strangers examining the headstones in the churchyard but I didn't give it much thought, being distracted in my role as the blushing bride. As in all Christian weddings, the priest—before marrying us—asked if anyone present had any objection to this marriage. One of the strangers interrupted the wedding, by standing up and saying that he had an objection! He astonished us by claiming that Mr Rochester already had a wife—a Creole woman, who he had married in Jamaica—who was still alive! Rochester admitted that this was true, but said that his wife—his accuser's sister—had gone mad. He then asked the gathering to come and see for themselves that he was speaking the truth.

When the gathering had walked up to the third floor of the house, Mr Rochester opened a curtain to reveal his wife, Bertha. It was the same savage woman who had torn my veil!

Bertha tried to bite Mr Rochester, and he said, 'This is the only loving embrace I have ever got from her.'

Later, Mr Rochester told me his life story. 'My father left his money to my brother Rowland, and made a match for me with Bertha, who was to inherit a massive fortune. She looked beautiful and I married her not knowing that her mother was locked up in an asylum for the insane. We lived in Jamaica for a while, but Bertha also went mad in due time and, in desperation, I returned to England to regain my sanctity.'

Then, Mr Rochester again asked me to marry him, but I refused.

'As long as Bertha is alive I will be seen as only your mistress,' I said.

I left Thornfield without telling anyone and wandered about till my money ran out. One night, just when I thought I could no longer go on, I saw a light in the distance. I dragged myself towards it, hoping against hope that it was a candle in a house, and that the residents would let me in. To my good fortune, the family that lived there welcomed me and made me feel at home. The man of the house was St John Rivers, and his two sisters were Diana and Mary.

My life there was a happy one and it became happier when one

day St John revealed to me that his full name was St John Eyre Rivers! He was my cousin and so were his two sisters! At last, I had found a family of my own. My happiness knew no bounds. But I did not reveal my true identity to them.

I said, 'My name is Jane Elliott.'

Then came great news about my Uncle John via a solicitor's letter that St John received. My uncle had left a certain Jane Eyre the astonishing sum of 20,000 pounds! I at once decided that the four of us would share this money equally—and also told them I was Jane Eyre!

St John revealed to me that he intended to become a clergyman. His ambition was to travel to India as a missionary. He began to get close to me but I did not love him and told him so, when he asked me to marry him and go to India with him. I said I would go with him but marriage was out of the question. He got very upset.

St John continued to press me to marry him in the following days to the extent that I almost said 'Yes'. But then, one night, I got a premonition that something terrible had happened to Mr Rochester.

I took a coach to Thornfield as soon as I could. When I reached there a terrible sight greeted me. The place was in ruins, completely burned down.

I learned that Bertha, in one of her fits, had burned down the house, and flung herself to her death in the flames. Mr Rochester saved his servants, but got badly burnt in the process: he lost his eyesight, and one of his hands. He was now living in a house called Ferndean, deep in the forest with two loyal servants.

I travelled immediately to Ferndean and told Mary, the servant, to hand me the tray she was about to give Mr Rochester. He sensed someone else was in the room and when I said it was me, he was overjoyed.

I told Mr Rochester everything that had happened after I left Thornfield, emphasizing that I did not love St John. He asked me to marry him and I agreed now as Bertha was no longer there. We were quietly married with only the priest and his assistant as witnesses.

I wrote to Diana and Mary and they were thrilled, though they did not mention what St John felt about my marriage. I also visited Adèle at her school and found out that she was unhappy there. Remembering my own awful school days, I took Adèle out of her school and admitted her to a good one.

Two years later, Mr Rochester began to regain his sight, just in time to see our first child—our newborn son. My cousins, Mary and Diana, also made happy marriages, and St John went to India to do missionary work as he had always wanted.

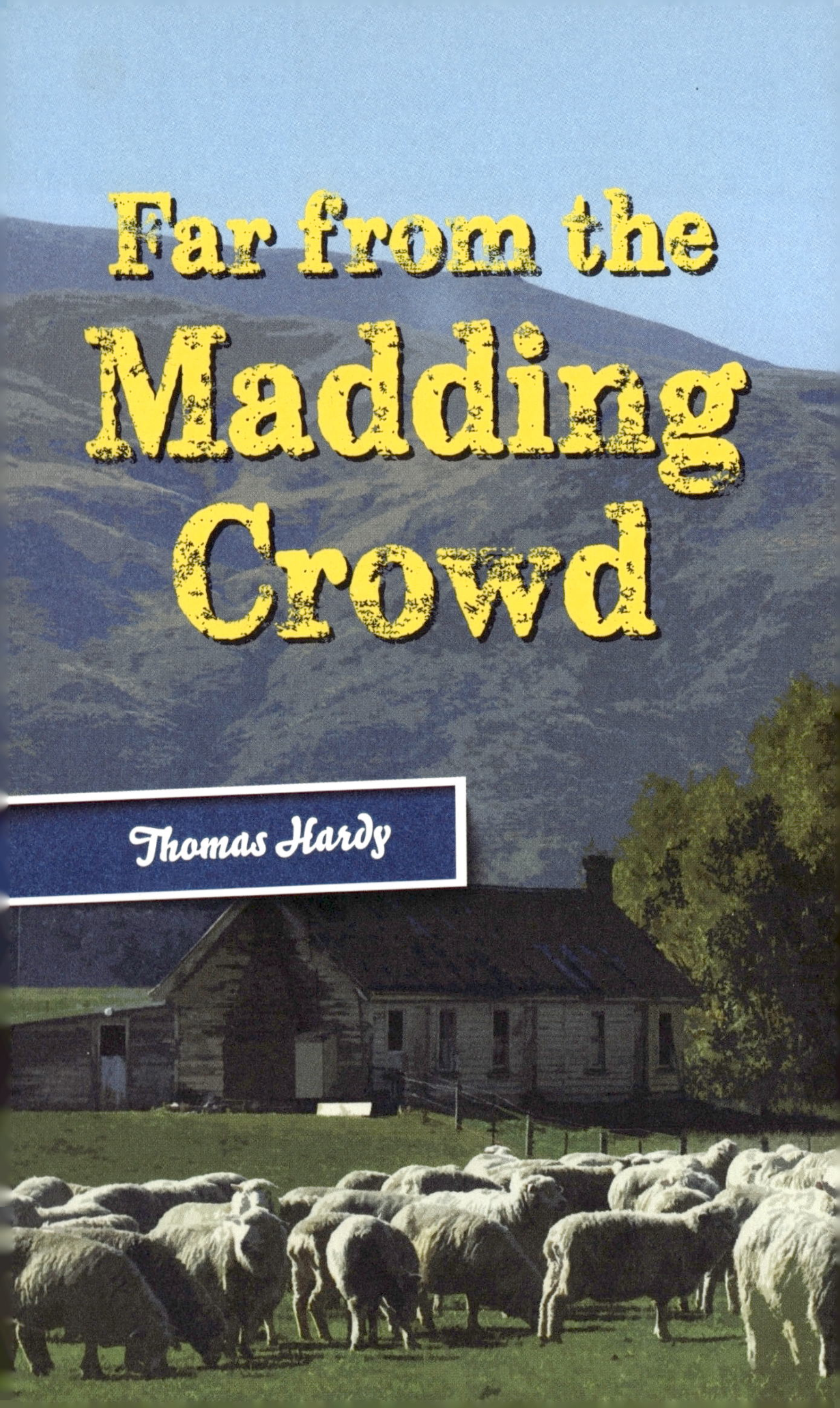
Far from the
Madding
Crowd
Thomas Hardy

His name was Gabriel but he was known as Farmer Oak—a name he had acquired when he rented a small farm and stocked it with 200 sheep. He had been a bailiff for some time and had helped his father tend the sheep of large farm owners before that.

When Gabriel smiled, the corners of his mouth rose up to meet his ears, his eyes crinkled, and the wrinkles around his eyes and mouth looked like a child's sketch of the rising sun. Throughout the week, he was a man of sound judgement, graceful movement, proper dress and general good character, neither moral nor immoral. At church on Sunday, however, Gabriel was distracted, and his mind drifted to what he would eat for dinner when the priest was giving his sermon. Even though he wore his best clothes to church, his neighbours always thought of him as in his work clothes and a felt hat.

His leather boots and leggings were rather large, which gave his feet plenty of room to manoeuvre. He carried with him a watch that resembled a small clock, which was many years older than Mr Oak's grandfather and which

tended to go either too slow or too fast! He was twenty-eight years old and a bachelor.

One morning, while on the Norcombe Hill ridge, Farmer Oak spied a colourful wagon approaching. The wagoner was walking alongside the two horses that drew the vehicle. An attractive young woman sat on top of the household goods—chairs and tables, an oak sofa, potted plants and a canary in a cage—that were piled up on the wagon. There was also a cat which lay quietly in a basket. The girl opened a looking glass and smiled at herself in the mirror; Oak had not yet come into her sight. Oak walked towards the gate at the turnpike and as he approached the toll booth he overheard a fight. It appeared to be a dispute between the wagon owner and the man at the toll booth that arose from the payment of two pence.

The wagoner told the toll booth man, 'Mistress won't pay more than two pence,' to which the former replied that then she can't pass.

'Shut the toll gate.'

Oak then came forward and gave the gatekeeper two pence more and told the keeper to allow the lady to pass. The young woman looked at Oak—whose features were not exactly beautiful but not quite ugly. She didn't speak to him and told her wagoner to proceed. As they left, the gatekeeper remarked that the woman was pretty, Oak replied that she had her faults which he summed up in one word—'Vanity'.

***

One day, Gabriel came upon two women milking a cow.

The younger of the two said, 'I wish we were rich; we could hire a man to do this work!'

'We aren't rich so we have to do the work ourselves,' her older companion, who happened to be her aunt, replied.

The young woman then exclaimed that the wind

had blown her hat over the ridge. Gabriel was standing at quite a height away from them over the ridge, and heard this exchange, even though he could not see the women. He picked up the hat that had flown near him. Then, the younger woman removed her cloak, Gabriel realized that she was the same person who had come in the colourful wagon, the lady who refused to pay the extra two pence at the booth and which Oak had paid. It was getting dark and when the ladies took up their lantern and departed, Gabriel also went back to his sheep, still in possession of the girl's hat.

When they met the next day, Gabriel told the young woman that he had found a hat.

'It's mine,' she said, while suppressing a smile.

'Your name's Farmer Oak, right? Do you have a large farm?' she then asked, swinging her black hair back.

He replied that it was about 100 acres. For five days the woman came to milk the cow but not once did her vision wander in Oak's direction.

One day, Gabriel Oak fell asleep in his small hut. He slept deeply and did not know for how long for when he awoke his head ached, his body felt numb and his dog was howling. And he felt soft hands loosening the handkerchief around his neck! It was the young woman. Gabriel had forgotten to open the ventilation before falling asleep in front of the fire, and would have died of suffocation if his dog had not alerted the girl to the expected danger. She had opened the door and, since there was no water, poured the milk she was carrying on him to rouse him.

Gabriel wiped his face and shook himself dry.

'How can I thank you?' he asked, gratefully.

'Oh, never mind,' the girl replied, and told him how his dog had pulled her by the skirt when she had come to do the milking.

'You saved my life, miss, and I do not even know your name!' Farmer Oak said.

'I'd rather not tell it. There is no reason either why I should, as you probably will never have much to do with me,' the girl answered.

'My name is Gabriel Oak,' the farmer said.

To which the girl replied,'You must like your own name very much to say it so easily. I always think mine is odd.'

Then, she challenged him to discover her name and left.

Gabriel learned that her name was Bathsheba Everdene. He also learned that the cow would finish giving milk in seven days. Oak feared the eighth day; and when it came, Bathsheba Everdene came up the hill no more.

Gabriel liked the name 'Bathsheba' and repeated it to himself when he was alone. He was soon in love with her, and decided to marry her.

'I'll make her my wife, or I shall be good for nothing!' he said to himself. And so, he began to find reasons to visit the cottage where Bathsheba's aunt, Mrs Hurst, lived.

The opportunity came when a ewe died, leaving behind a lamb. He carried the lamb in a basket to Bathsheba's house with the intention of gifting it to her and asking her hand in marriage. Since she wasn't at home, he revealed his plans to her aunt. The older woman told him that she had many suitors, which turned out to be untrue. However, Bathsheba turned him down. When he pressed her for a reason, she said she didn't want to marry someone who she did not love. Gabriel tried once more to convince her, but eventually accepted her answer, and left in a dignified manner.

Sometime later, Bathsheba inherited an uncle's farm in Weatherbury, and left. The news of her departure affected Farmer Oak greatly but something else happened which would have a great bearing on his future life. He awoke at dawn one morning, to hear the tinkling sound of his sheep's bells moving quickly, as if the animals were rushing somewhere together.

He raced down the road and ran up the hill—and found all his sheep missing. They had disappeared! The farmer gave his shepherd's call but did not get one bleat in reply. When he inspected the hedge, he found a gap in it and saw sheep's footprints. When he looked over the

cliff he saw a terrible sight—200 muddled sheep carcasses. Since the animals were not insured, all of Oak's savings had disappeared at a single blow. Apparently his sheep dog, enthusiastic after eating a dead ewe which Oak had fed him, drove the poor creatures across the hedge and over the cliff.

Two months later, Farmer Oak landed in the town of Casterbridge, where he sought employment as a bailiff. His sad incident had left its scar on him but had also given him a dignified calm that he never possessed before. Since nobody wanted a bailiff—all the farmers seemed to be wanting shepherds—Oak got a shepherd's crook for two shillings, and exchanged his overcoat for shepherd's clothing.

Now that he looked like a shepherd, Oak mingled with other farm people and learned that there was another fair at Shottsford the following day. When he learned that this town was close to Weatherbury, his ears pricked up. Weatherbury! The place where Bathsheba went two months back! The information turned his night into noon. Oak then did what he thought was best—he hopped into a wagon that was travelling to Weatherbury and fell asleep. When he awoke he heard voices speaking about a woman with 'a fine body, but who was a devil inside,' and 'she's a vain person,' and 'she's not married'. Oak thought they would be referring to Bathsheba, though he wasn't too sure about it. He slipped out of the wagon at Weatherbury and some half mile away saw a building on fire.

Oak leaped over the gate and raced towards the blazing fire. The farmer saw that the fire had started in a rick-yard. His experience as a farmer served him well.

He shouted to the person closest to him, 'Cut off the draught beneath the wheat rick. Quick, get a tarpaulin.'

A rick cloth was brought; it prevented the flames from entering below the stack of corn and burnt in a vertical position.

'Get the water bucket here, keep on pouring water on the cloth.'

Oak then called for a ladder and when he learned that the ladder had been burnt completely, he himself climbed up the stack and with his crook beat off the fiery rubble.

Two women appeared from the farmhouse, one on foot and the other on a horse.

'He certainly is a shepherd,' said the former. 'His crook is shining as he hits the rick… His dress has two burnt holes, I do say! He sure is a fine shepherd, ma'am.'

There were whispers around, 'Whose shepherd is he?'

'Does anyone know his name?'
'Wish he were a shepherd on this farm!'

As the fire died off, Gabriel Oak got off from his perch.

The girl on the horse said, 'Maryann, tell the shepherd that the farmer wants to express thanks for the huge service he has done.'

Maryann met Oak and passed on this message to him. She told him that the owner of the farm, which was called Upper Farm, was a rich woman.

Oak advanced to the girl in the saddle, raised his hat in a respectful manner, and asked the woman who had a woollen veil over her face if she needed a shepherd. She lifted her veil, and Oak realized he was once again facing Bathsheba Everdene. When she did not speak, he repeated his question.

Bathsheba did not know whether to be amused by this unexpected meeting or to be anxious about its awkwardness. She was not embarrassed and she remembered how Oak had professed his love for her two months back.

Anyway, in reply to Gabriel's query, she said 'Yes'.

After Bathsheba's bailiff drew up a legal contract, Oak decided to look for lodging. One of the men directed him to Walter's Malt

House. On his way there, Gabriel ran into a poor girl with an attractive voice. He asked her for directions, and she told him which way to go. She seemed to be hiding something but rather than pursue the matter, Gabriel promised to keep their encounter a secret and gave her a shilling—for she seemed to need it—before they parted ways.

At the Malt House, Gabriel Oak met many of the local men, one of whom promised him lodging. The owner of the House, Mr Smallbury, happened to know Oak's grandparents so Gabriel was treated very well. He drank the liquor they offered him and got to know, among other people, the Malster's sons, Jacob and William (aged sixty-five and forty, respectively), a cheerful gentleman named Mark Clark, Henry Fray—who always signed his name as 'Henery'—and Jan Coggan who was well-known in and around Weatherbury having been chief witness and best man at numerous unions during the past twenty years.

Gabriel learned that Bathsheba had inherited the farm after her uncle, a bachelor, died suddenly. When he enquired about her, they said they did not know much about the new mistress, since she had only come to town recently.

'But the family is a good one,' they said.

Suddenly there was a stir in the house with news that Bathsheba had caught her bailiff, Pennyways, stealing half a bushel of barley. He then confessed to having stolen five bushels earlier, when she said that she would not prosecute him if he confessed.

But Susan Tall's husband entered in a tearing hurry, and asked if they had heard the news about Miss Everdene's maid, Fanny Robin.

'She can't be found. And she left the farm in her house clothes!'

The men arose and went to the farm where Bathsheba told them to begin a search for Fanny in the morning. Jacob Smallbury then asked if someone was courting her.

'She was seeing a man in Casterbridge … a soldier,' Maryann replied from the window.

William Smallbury said he could go to Casterbridge barracks and find out.

Bathsheba agreed to this plan, 'If she does not return tomorrow.'

At Coggan's that night Gabriel Oak reflected upon his new life. He also thought of his plans for bringing his few utensils and books from Norcombe.

The next morning, the good-looking and rich Farmer Boldwood presented himself at Bathsheba's farm, but Bathsheba declined to meet him, for she was not properly dressed. She later learnt that he had enquired about Fanny Robin.

'Why should he inquire about Fanny?' Bathsheba asked Mrs Coggan, who was her housekeeper.

'Oh, because, as she had no friends in her childhood, he took her and put her to school, and got her placed here under your uncle,' Mrs Coggan replied.

Later, Gabriel Oak presented himself at Bathsheba's farm, ready for his new job. All the men were there, and the farm owner paid them their salaries, one by one. She proved herself to be an astute person. First, she declared that the bailiff had been dismissed

for being a thief and that henceforth she would handle all matters herself.

Then she asked if there was any news of Fanny Robin and got a 'nothing' in reply. Jacob Smallbury said that he and Farmer Boldwood had stopped by the millpond in case she was drowned there but they had found nothing.

Laban Tall said, 'The new shepherd went to Buck's Head but nobody has seen her.'

Bathsheba further learned that William Smallbury had gone to Casterbridge and would be back shortly. When he did return, William told them that the soldiers had left the town but he came to know that Fanny had a relationship with one of the officers.

Henry Fray said that the new shepherd would require an assistant and so a lad named Cain Ball was entrusted with that job.

It was ten o'clock at night, many miles away from Weatherbury, at a military station on the outskirts of a town. A small figure was walking towards the garrison. When the figure reached the military station, it spoke a series of words as if remembering '… one… two…three' and stopping at 'five'. Then balls of snow were seen flying through the air towards the military station. The person throwing them apparently had very poor aim, and a weak arm, for they were way off target.

But after several attempts, one snowball hit the target and a man's face peeped out from the fifth window and he asked who it was. His voice did not show any surprise.

A girl's voice asked, 'Is that Sergeant Troy?' and got a positive answer.

'Frank, it's me, Fanny Robin.'

'Fanny!' the man exclaimed, astonished. 'How did you get to this place? I was not expecting you.'

The girl said, 'I hope you are not angry with me. Frank, when shall we get married? Can you meet me now.'

'Dear Fanny, No! I don't have any leave and the night bugle has been blown.'

'Frank, I love you. You told me many times that you would marry me.'

'I will,' Frank answered and told Fanny not to cry for she had begun to sob.

'I'll leave now ... meet me tomorrow at North Street at Mrs Twills's.'

'I'll meet you my dear...goodnight,' Sergeant Frank Troy answered.

It was in the corn market that Bathsheba came across Farmer Boldwood. She was with Liddy Smallbury and the latter pointed out Boldwood to her, since she had met him when Boldwood had come to their farm. At the market, Boldwood did not seem to notice them at all; in fact he brushed past them while exiting without giving them so much as a glance.

On Sunday, Liddy asked her mistress, 'Did you see what Mr Boldwood did in this morning in church, Miss?'

Bathsheba replied rather indifferently, 'No. What did the farmer do?'

'He did not look at you even once,' replied Liddy.

Bathsheba suddenly said, 'I forgot completely about the Valentine I bought.'

'For Farmer Boldwood?' asked Liddy.

'No, no. It's for Teddy Coggan who I had promised something,' said Bathsheba and drew out an elaborate and attractive Valentine from her drawer and wrote a message which ran: 'Roses are red; violets are blue; carnations are sweet; just like you.'

Suddenly Liddy said, 'Why not send it to Boldwood?'

Bathsheba thought it would be funny and decided to toss up a hymn book to see who it would go to: if it fell down shut, the card would go to Boldwood; if it fell open, to Teddy. The card fell down shut and so it was posted to Boldwood—

and Bathsheba added on the seal in red, in jest, two words 'Marry Me'.

Thus, in an unplanned and idle way, the deed was done.

On the evening of Valentine's Day, Boldwood ate his supper as usual and reflected on the day's happening. The words 'Marry Me', rang through his mind countless times. The letter had a motive and an origin, he reminded himself. For the hundredth time, he reread those two little words. At dawn the next day, he dressed and left his house and as he walked towards the east, the van with the post came in his sight. He hurried towards it as if another letter or parcel awaited him. There was a letter, but it was addressed to the new shepherd at Weatherbury Farm. Boldwood took it and told the courier that he would deliver it to the shepherd himself, for he spied Oak on the hill right then. The latter was heading to the Malt House and Boldwood followed him there.

Upon entering the place, Boldwood went up to Gabriel and told him about the letter, after apologizing that he had opened it.

Oak read the letter which began 'Dear Friend' and was written by an unknown hand. In short, the letter thanked Gabriel for the shilling he gave the girl one evening and which she was returning now. She said that everything was fine with her now and she would be marrying a sergeant from the 11th Dragoon Guards called Troy. It was signed, 'Your well wisher, Fanny Robin'. It was the poor girl with an attractive voice; Gabriel had bumped into her when first going to the Malt House!

Mr Boldwood explained that Troy was a cunning romantic chap whose mother was a French governess, who had an attachment with a certain (late) Lord Severn. Her husband was a poor doctor who lost his best friends and her son had to work as a lawyer's second clerk in Casterbridge. Then he joined the army.

He added, 'Fanny is a very silly girl!'

Boldwood opened the pocket-book and asked Gabriel, in a careless manner, if he could recognize the handwriting.

Oak glanced into the book, and replied instantly, with a flushed face, 'Miss Everdene's.' 'Bathsheba's.' The lonely farmer then went home,

feeling rather ashamed that he had revealed his feelings to a stranger.

In the barrack town there were two churches—the All Saints' and the All Souls'. Had Miss Fanny Robin gone to the All Saints'—where Sergeant Troy would be waiting to make her his wife as he had promised her—our tale would have taken a vastly different turn. But she waited for him at All Souls'. At All Saints' the smartly dressed army officer waited patiently for his lady love to show up. As the time passed without Fanny's arrival, Sergeant Troy got quite upset. He left the church and crossed the road towards a square when he ran into Fanny.

He suppressed his hurt feelings and simply said, 'Well!'

'I went to the wrong church, dear Frank! I wasn't frightened though. May be we could get married tomorrow?' she asked.

But Troy was angry. He called her a fool and said emphatically that 'tomorrow' would not come for some time!

'God knows!' he said when Fanny asked him when they would marry.

Boldwood eventually called upon Bathsheba, at the sheep washing pool one day.

There he told her, 'Miss Everdene, I wish to marry you. I'm forty-one years old and was a confirmed bachelor, until I met you. I wish to make you my wife.'

Bathsheba told Farmer Boldwood that she had not yet 'fallen in love with him', and wanted till harvest time to give him an answer.

While pondering over this possibility, Bathsheba went up to Gabriel and asked him what the other workers of the farm felt about her appearing and talking with Boldwood. When Gabriel replied that it was 'unworthy of a comely woman', the two began to quarrel. Bathsheba told Gabriel that he was jealous and ordered the shepherd to leave the farm. Gabriel readily agreed.

It wasn't too long before Bathsheba needed the services of Gabriel Oak urgently. Hardly twenty-four hours had passed, when several farm workers rushed to Miss Everdene and told her that seventy sheep had broken the fence and wandered into a field of young clover. Only Gabriel knew how to save the sheep which would be bloated from eating the clover. But he wasn't willing to return—until Bathsheba wrote him a note pleading, 'Gabriel, don't desert me.' Within fifteen minutes, Gabriel was among the sick sheep, using a small tube called a trochar like an expert surgeon. Soon all the sheep were saved.

June arrived and it was time to shear the sheep. Led by Gabriel, the men did the job in less than half an hour. Bathsheba noticed the feat and praised Gabriel for it. Inwardly, Gabriel was thrilled and worked eagarly as ever. Suddenly, he spotted Farmer Boldwood in the farthest corner of the barn. Boldwood greeted Bathsheba in low inaudible tones, and soon Bob Coggan was leading out her horse. In his discomfort, Gabriel injured the sheep he was shearing. Bathsehba severely scolded him for it.

She and Boldwood then climbed their steeds and, as the two rode away, a worker said, 'This means marriage.'

That evening Boldwood visited the Upper Farm and had a talk in private with Bathsheba. But even as she promised to reconsider his marriage proposal in a 'few weeks', she did not give him a definite answer.

One evening, Bathsheba was on her rounds when she bumped into someone whose spur got stuck in her dress.The two spoke to each other and when her lantern opened up she discovered that it was a soldier and not an intruder as she had suspected. Indeed it was Troy and he immediately charmed her by commenting on her beauty. Troy used the word 'beauty' several times in their conversation and when finally they got disentangled, Bathsheba asked Liddy about the man and learned that it was Sergeant Troy. She regretted being rude to him.

Troy was a charming and romantic fellow. Bathsheba next saw him with the haymakers in her field where he offered her the gift of a gold watch—which she refused. But as their intimacy increased and he appeared again on the farm and told her about the well-known sword exercise that soldiers are so skilled at. After he gave her an impressive exhibition of swordsmanship, Troy kissed Bathsheba—and disappeared. Miss Everdene had fallen in love with the soldier.

Bathsheba met Boldwood on her way to Liddy's one evening when he reminded her of the Valentine. She explained that it was done in jest and went on to tell Boldwood that she loved Troy and had even kissed him. The ferocity with which Boldwood greeted this news scared Bathsheba. She was determined to meet Troy to warn him of approaching danger. She followed Troy to Bath where he told her he would be going, to tell him not to come back to Weatherbury. Two weeks went

by and a farmer said he saw Bathsheba go to a park with a soldier, hand in hand.

That night Bathsheba returned to the farm. Boldwood was also present, as was Sergeant Troy. Boldwood attempted to bribe Troy into marrying Fanny Robin, but Troy showed Boldwood a newspaper cutting which revealed that he had already married Bathsheba.

***

Gabriel again came to Bathsheba's rescue when a fierce storm hit the farm. As he helped to save the wheat bales, Bathsheba confessed to the shepherd that she had not intended to marry Troy but had gave in to his charms as she was caught between distraction and jealousy.

Two months later, Troy and Bathsheba travelled up Yalbury Hill. Troy had quit the army and was dressed in fashionable farmer's clothing. While Bathsheba complained about the money he had lost at the races, he told her that she had 'lost all her sauciness'. On the way, they came across a woman who asked Troy for directions to Casterbridge. When Troy spoke, the woman, Fanny

Robin, cried out aloud and fell to the ground. Troy stayed back to speak to her and sent the horse and Bathsheba up the hill. Troy told Fanny he would meet her in two days' time. Then, he and Bathsheba had an argument, for Bathesheba had realized who the woman was. Meanwhile, after a painful walk all night, Fanny reached Casterbridge.

Meanwhile, Bathsheba found a strand of yellow hair in Troy's watch and faced him with it. Troy readily replied that it belonged to a girl he had once loved. Bathsheba broke down into tears.

The following day, one of Bathsheba's employees gave her some tragic news. Joseph Poorgrass said Fanny Robin had died, and he did not know how. Bathsheba suspected that the girl had died giving birth to Troy's baby. She told Poorgrass that she would bury the body and sent him to bring Fanny home.

On the coffin was the inscription, 'Fanny and Child'. When the coffin was brought to the farm, Gabriel Oak erased the words 'and Child' from it.

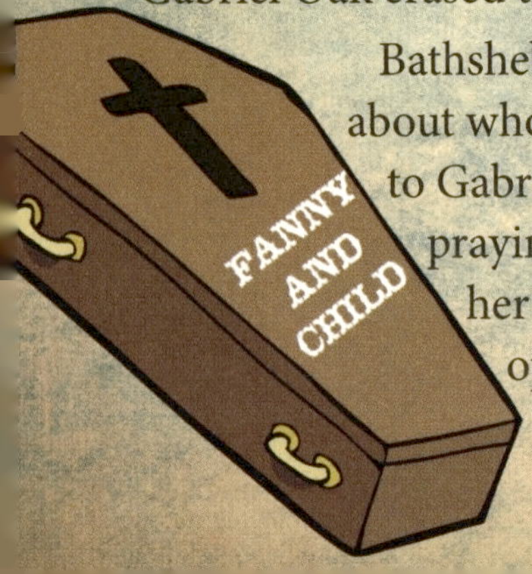

Bathsheba, now utterly confused about who exactly had died, went to Gabriel's house and found him praying. When he did not give her straight answers, she pried opened the coffin herself—and saw the child and mother, whose hair was yellow. She decided to wait for Troy to return.

When Troy returned, he shocked Bathsheba by telling her that he was not morally hers. He declared that, in the eyes of Heaven, Fanny was his wife, since she had had his baby. Bathsheba ran away from the house in despair. Soon, Troy too departed from the place.

One day, Bathsheba was in the market when a stranger brought her some sad news.
He had been walking near the river, he said, and had found Troy's clothes lying on the bank.

'His clothes were there, Mistress, but there was no sign of him. I fear he may have drowned while swimming,' he said, giving her his clothes.

The watch still had the strand of Fanny's yellow hair caught in it.

Bathsheba refused to believe the news.

'No, it is not true; it cannot be true!' she said, and would not listen to anything more on the matter.

In the following months, Gabriel acquired increasing success. Bathsheba gave up control of Upper Farm and allowed Gabriel to

oversee it. In his despair over Bathsheba, Boldwood had neglected his farm and therefore lost much of his wealth. So, he hired Gabriel to help him out, and paid him a portion of the profits. Gabriel also got a horse and became bailiff for both farms. Eventually, Boldwood gave him a larger part of the farm, since he wanted to retire from actively managing the farm.

Meanwhile, Bathsheba was still unwilling to believe that Troy was dead, and Boldwood was living in the hope that Bathsheba would marry him once the six-year waiting period—required to declare a person dead—ended.

Bathsheba had been right. Troy was not dead. He was wandering in England and America, working with a circus. Once, when the circus was touring England, Troy happened to see Boldwood and Bathsheba. The two of them did not recognize him due to his disguise. Attracted by her wealth, Troy decided to return to Bathsheba. Boldwood had also become more persistent in courting Bathsheba, but she kept putting him off.

Things came to a head at Boldwood's Christmas Eve party. The guests arrived, all dressed in their finest. Again, Boldwood asked Bathsheba to marry him. He gave her a ring and asked her to wear it, 'at least for that night only'.

Bathsheba agreed reluctantly. At that moment, Troy turned up.

'I have come back for you, Bathsheba,' he said.

Bathsheba took a step back. This angered Troy. Suddenly, there was a scream, and a gunshot. Boldwood had killed Troy and would have shot himself too, if a worker had not stopped him. Troy was buried in the same grave as Fanny Robin.

During the murder trial, it turned out that Boldwood had stocked closets full of expensive ladies clothes and jewellery, which were marked 'Bathsheba Boldwood'. The judge sentenced him to death. However, the citizens of Weatherbury convinced the Home Secretary that he was not fully responsible for his actions, and got his sentence commuted to a life in prison.

Bathsheba Everdene's spirits revived with the arrival of spring. She bumped into Gabriel, who was singing in the church choir. When he told her he was planning to leave Weatherbury, she asked him to 'please stay' for she was indeed courting his love.

A few months later, Gabriel Oak married Bathsheba Everdene in a small ceremony. Later, the couple hosted a dinner for the villagers who sang loudly for their happiness and prosperity.

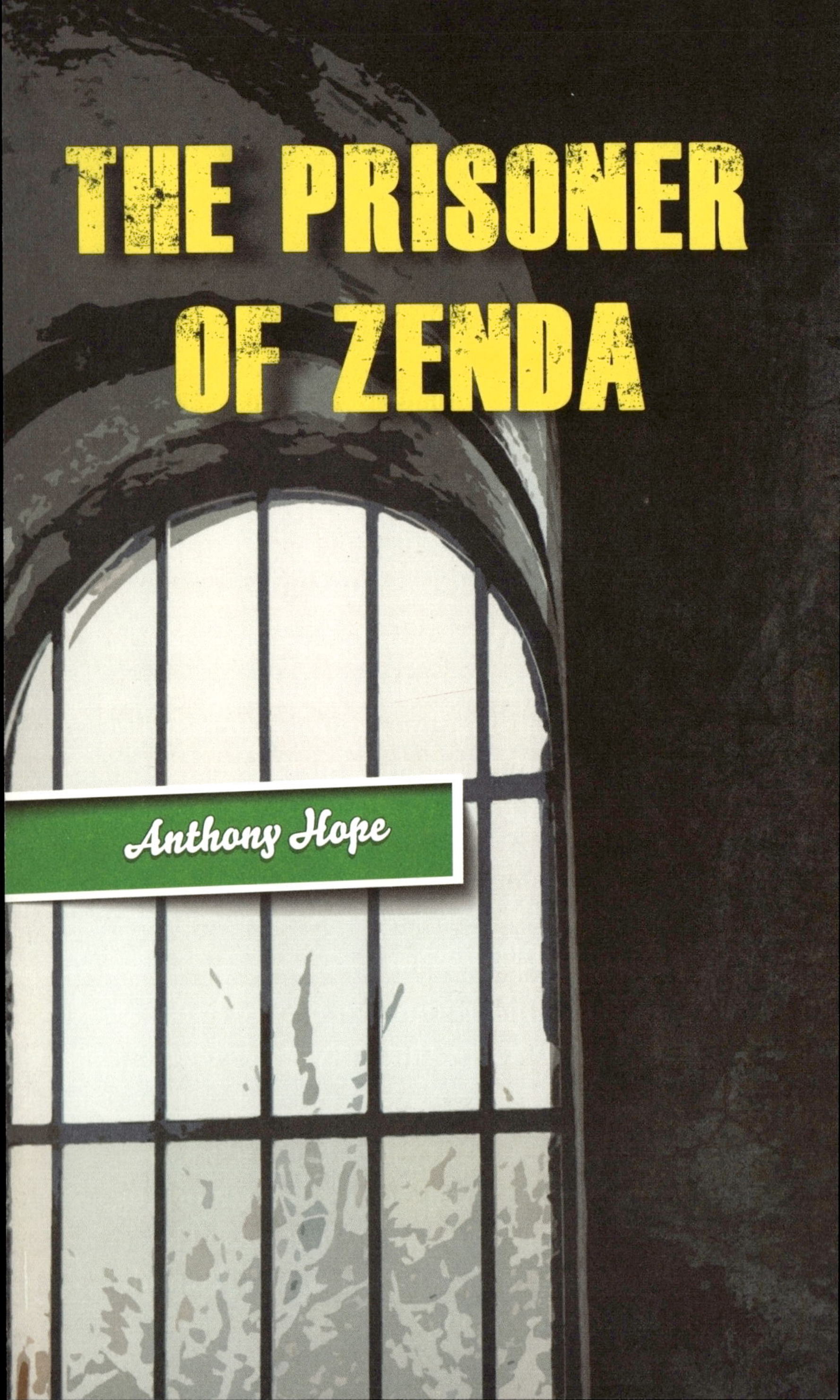
THE PRISONER
OF ZENDA
Anthony Hope

One morning, during breakfast, my sister-in-law asked me, 'Rudolf, when are you going to do something?'

I put down my egg spoon and said, 'Rose dear, why should I do anything? I am in a comfortable position, both financially and socially. Indeed, my place in society is fortunate. My brother is Lord Robert Burlesdon, and his countess is my charming sister-in-law. That surely is enough, I must say.'

The countess persisted, 'You're twenty-nine years old and have not done anything…'

'I don't need to do anything,' I responded, but Rose got quite upset with this remark. You see, her family's social standing cannot match that of the Rassendylls. But, her good looks aside, she has a big fortune and Robert quite wisely overlooked her ancestry.

Rose remarked, 'Good families normally are worse than other families.'

As I ran my fingers through my red hair, she cried, 'I'm so happy that Robert has black hair!'

Robert made his entry just then. He was a man who awoke at seven o'clock in the morning and completed his work before breakfast. He patted his wife's cheek, which was a bit red and asked her, 'What's wrong?'

I said, in a tone that reflected that I was hurt, 'Rose doesn't like my red hair or the fact that I don't work for a living.'

My brother said, 'In our family, red hair is a once-in-a-generation thing, and he got it; like his long nose.'

When Rose said she didn't quite like both and the reason for it, I said I did like it and looked up to a picture of Aunt Amelia hanging on the wall. My sister-in-law did not like that either.

As I got back to my egg I commented, 'I like being a member of the Elphberg clan.'

Now, I realize that I owe you—dear readers—an explanation. It is important that I tell you just why Rose was upset with my hair and nose, and why I dared to refer to myself as an Elphberg. Eminent they have been for long, but the Rassendylls cannot boast of being connected to the Royal House or being grander than the Elphbergs.

So, I must dig up the scandal that Lady Burlesdon wants to forget. In 1733, in George II's reign, when he and the Prince of Wales were not yet unfriendly to each other, a certain prince visited the English Court. History says that he was

Ruritania's Rudolf the Third. A handsome and tall young man, he had an unusually sharp and long nose and red hair—indeed, the hair and nose that have marked out the Elphbergs.

After staying in England for some months, this Prince fought a duel with a famous English nobleman, the husband of an extremely beautiful wife. The Prince Rudolf suffered severe wounds and was quietly smuggled away by the ambassador of Ruritania. The English nobleman was unhurt in the duel but he caught a severe chill as the duel was fought in very cold weather and passed away several months after Prince Rudolf departed. Some months later the Englishman's wife gave birth to an heir to the Burlesdon title, estates and family. This wife was Countess Amelia, whose portrait hung in the Park Lane house drawing room. Aunt Amelia's husband was James, the fifth Earl of Burlesdon and twenty-second Baron Rassendyll.

Rudolf returned to Ruritania, got married and became king of his country. His descendants have reigned continuously, except for one, brief interval. If you look at the fifty-odd pictures at the Burlesdon galleries of the last 150 years, you'll find five or six long-nosed redheads, including the sixth Earl. These descendants have blue eyes too, while the Rassendylls have mostly dark eyes.

I would like to mention that I studied in a German school and university, and could speak German as easily as I could English. I was also comfortable in French, and knew a bit of Spanish and Italian. I was also a good shot and a fine swordsman, I could ride most four-legged creatures and I had a cool head beneath my flaming red hair. My parents left me 2,000 pounds a year and nature that urged me to roam. My sister-in-law says that I seek opportunities, while my brother recognizes his duties.

My answer to that was, 'Opportunities, indeed, are duties.'

Rose went on, 'Now, Sir Jacob Borrodaile has the perfect job for you. He'll soon be heading an Embassy, and Robert says he is sure that he'll take you as an attaché. Do take it, Rudolf—to please me.'

Now, when my sister-in-law puts things that way, twisting her dainty hands and wrinkling her pretty eyebrows, I begin to have second thoughts. Besides, I thought it would a good idea to pass my time in the position she suggested.

So I said, 'If no unexpected obstacle arises, and if Sir Jacob gives me an offer, I will go along with him!'

Robert got me the offer, and I made the promise. However, it would be six months before Sir Jacob would take up his assignment. To pass those months, I decided to journey to Ruritania.

I had never been there and my father never encouraged me to go there. And my brother (egged on by Rose) felt that I must maintain the family tradition and stay away from Ruritania. So, I lied to them and told them that I would be visiting the Tyrol region and would write a book about it when I returned. They loved the idea. However, I did not have the slightest intention of putting pen to paper my experiences in Ruritania, even it was a country which had played a big role in European history and where—according to The Times—Rudolf V would shortly be crowned king.

***

My uncle William always believed that all men passing through Paris must spend twenty-four hours there. So I got a room at The Continental, and after visiting George Featherly at the Embassy and dropping in to the Opera, I went to meet Bertram Bertrand, a fairly reputed poet and the Paris correspondent of a leading magazine.

While Bertram was surrounded by pleasant fellows, he himself seemed down and out. So I tried to rally him and after fencing with me for some time, he exclaimed, 'I'm in love—in love!'

'Give it up, Bert. She leaves Paris tomorrow,' said George—who was standing by—with an unkind smile.

'I know that,' Bertram snapped, 'I know.'

I ventured to ask, 'Who are you talking about?'

George said, 'Antoinette de Mauban.'

A rich, handsome and reputedly ambitious widow, the lady was a celebrity of sorts. So I asked where she was off to.

George smiled cruelly at Bertram but answered me in a pleasant tone, 'We don't know. Bert, I must tell you I met an eminent man at her place some nights back. Have you met the Duke of Strelsau?'

'I have,' Bertram replied sourly.

The duke in question was the son of the late King of Ruritania, and half-brother to the new King. He had, I was told, returned to Ruritania for the coronation.

George rubbed it in, 'Bert, don't worry! He will not marry fair Antoinette. But then, attention from royals is difficult to resist, right Rudolf?'

With a parting 'Confound you!' I returned to my hotel to catch my sleep.

***

George Featherly accompanied me to the station and, after I purchased a ticket to Dresden, who asked me with a grin if I was going to the movies.

Since George is a habitual gossip, I didn't risk telling him I was going to Ruritania, for then the news would have spread like wildfire.

He suddenly left me and darted off to greet a fashionably dressed and graceful woman who had appeared at the station. She was tall, had a full figure and was perhaps a bit over thirty. When George rejoined me, he told me that the lady was Antoinette de Mauban and was travelling to Dresden, like me.

After resting a night in Dresden, I resumed my journey to Ruritania. Madame de Mauban hopped onto that train as well. Knowing that she wanted to be left undisturbed, I completely avoided her but noticed that she remained on board.

Just before reaching Strelsau, I learned from the papers that the coronation had been brought forward, and would occur in a couple of days in Strelsau, the country's capital. Strelsau was flooded with visitors, and hotel rooms were all sold out. So I decided to take up lodging in Zenda, a town some fifty miles away, and stepped off the train at that station. I noticed that Madame de Mauban remained in the train. She obviously had secure apartments in Strelsau.

***

The inn I decided to stay at was run by a plump lady and her two daughters (who called the Duke 'Black Michael'). There, I ran into Johann, Duke Michael's forest guard. He was quite amazed at my crop of red hair, and asked if I was related to the King of Ruritania. Johann said that he had cancelled his plans of going go Strelsau for the coronation due to some work.

He said that he had planned to stay at the home of his sister, the wife of a rich trader in Strelsau. Now that he was not going, Johann invited me to take his place at his sister's house—an offer that I gladly accepted. The next morning, I decided to climb the hill leading to Black Michael's castle and the forest of Zenda. When I reached the forest, I propped myself against a big tree trunk, smoked a good cigar and dozed off. I awoke to someone exclaiming, 'Why! Give him a shave and he'll look just like the King!'

I looked up and saw two men dressed in shooting costumes and carrying guns, regarding me rather curiously. They said they were in the service of the King Ruritania.

I said I was Rudolf Rassendyll, from England.

One of the men, whose name was Colonel Sapt, whispered, 'Rassendyll….You're a Burlesdon?'

I replied that my brother was Lord Burlesdon.

'Your head has betrayed you,' he said laughingly, and asked his companion, Fritz von Tarlenheim, if he knew the story. From their conversation, I learned that apparently everyone in Ruritania knew the story.

Suddenly a sharp voice rang in the air. It was the King! When he appeared I was completely taken aback. He was almost a mirror-image of me (or I of him!)—except that I sported a beard and that he was half-an-inch shorter than me.

There were some other differences too. The King had a fleshier, more oval face than mine and I thought his mouth was not as firm as mine. Otherwise, our likeness to each other was remarkable.

The King's eyes twinkled and he burst out laughing. He greeted me as 'cousin', and said, 'You must forgive me if I was taken aback. A man doesn't expect to see double at this time of day, eh, Fritz?'

Fritz and Sapt both laughed.

'I hope I have not offended you,' I said.

The King laughed and asked me where I was going. When I said I was headed to Strelsau for the coronation, he smiled, but appeared to be slightly uneasy. Then, the humour of the situation got to him again and he broke out into merry laughter.

'Fritz, Fritz!' he cried, 'a thousand crowns for a sight of brother Michael's face when he sees a pair of us!'

'It may not be wise for Mr Rassendyll to visit Strelsau just now,' Fritz observed.

'Well, Sapt?' the King asked.

'He mustn't go,' the old man growled.

'Come now...' the King began to say but I interrupted him, and offered to leave Ruritania that very day.

However, the King insisted that I dine with him. So we set out to a lodge in the forest and started the feasting. The King and I then drank quite a bit of some excellent wine. He raised a toast to his 'Cousin Rudolf', and I raised my glass to the 'Elphberg Red'.

All of us drank like never before and talked like we never had in our lives, just like people who have drunk too much do. The King had just announced that he had drunk enough, when Josef entered the room with another bottle—a rare wine that the King's brother Michael, the Duke of Strelsau, had sent over especially for the King. When the King tasted it, he said I could ask him for anything—even half his kingdom—just not that wine. He drank straight from the bottle and did not stop until the bottle was empty. He then flung his arms and head on the table and fell asleep.

***

I don't know how long I slept, but I awoke at five o'clock, dripping wet and very annoyed. Old Sapt had poured a bucket of cold water on me! Fritz looked very pale and the King was lying on the floor, also soaking wet. The cheeky Sapt kicked even him, but it had no effect.

Fritz explained, 'We've been trying to wake him up for half an hour.'

'What about the coronation?' I asked.

We discussed the matter. We could not send word that the King was sick or drunk. And since the entire nation was present for the coronation it was a now-or-never situation. If the King did not make it to the coronation, Black Michael was sure to usurp his place.

Sept asked me, 'Was the King drugged?'

'Yes,' I said.

'That damned Black Michael!' Fritz cursed.

Sapt, his bushy brows knitted tightly, stood thinking for a while.

Then, he stared at me and said, 'Fate has sent you here and it now sends you to Strelsau. You must stand in for the King.'

At first I was shocked by his remark, but eventually agreed to take the King's place. Sapt outlined his plan.

'We will take up lodging in the Palace. When they leave us, we'll mount our steeds—Fritz will stay back to stand guard at the King's room—and ride quickly back here. The King will then be ready, and can return with me to Strelsau while you race away to the border.'

I nodded my comprehension.

Sapt then carried the King into the wine cellar. Johann's mother, who worked at the lodge, saw them but turned away without a word.

On Sapt's orders, Josef shaved off my moustache and beard. Fritz gazed at me and said, 'We'll do it!'

Then, I dressed in the King's clothes—the uniform of a colonel of the King's Guard. When Sapt came in to give me the King's sword, I asked Sapt what he had done to the old woman.

'I tied up her hands and legs, pushed a handkerchief in her mouth and locked her in the coal cellar, next to the king, just to be sure,' Sapt replied. 'Josef will take care of both of them.'

Fritz donned a captain's uniform while Sapt dressed up in his uniform. We rode off as soon as Josef said the horses were ready.

On the way, Sapt instructed me in details of the King's life, and promised to assist me at all times. Then, he asked if I was a Catholic. When I said I wasn't, he gave me some basic lessons in Roman Catholicism.

We reached the station and Fritz explained to the station master that the King had changed his plans. We entered a first-class carriage. I looked down at my watch—the King's watch—and saw that it was just eight o'clock. I wondered if the King's Guard would be looking for us.

'I hope they don't find the King,' Fritz replied nervously.

Sapt shrugged.

By half past nine, I saw the spires and towers of the great city. There was a great activity at the station. All manner of men were hurrying hither and thither, some to the church, others to Duke Michael's residence. The city's bells were ringing joyfully—their King had entered his capital!

As the crowd outside shouted, 'God save our King,' old Sapt smiled.

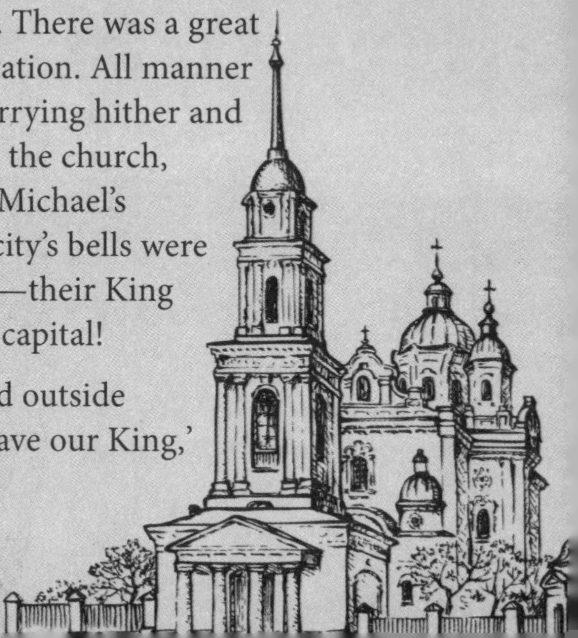

'God save them both!' he whispered. Then, he pressed my knee and said, 'Have courage, lad!'

***

A happy group of dignitaries and officers awaited me at the station. An elderly military gentleman, highly decorated with medals, stood at the head of this delegation. He wore the red and yellow ribbon of the Red Rose of Ruritania, which also ornamented my undeserving breast.

Sapt whispered, 'That's Marshal Strakencz,' who I knew was the most famous Ruritanian army veteran. Behind him stood the country's Chancellor, dressed in long robes.

After greeting me, the Marshal delivered an apology from the Duke of Strelsau, who could not come due to a sudden illness.

I met many more distinguished dignitaries and was happy to note that no one suspected who I really was. Suddenly, I noticed a pretty face staring at me—it was Antoinette de Mauban! She also looked surprised, but did not do anything wild—like screaming that I wasn't the King—so I managed to keep my cool.

We arrived at the Cathedral and, through misty eyes, I saw the heavily robed priests waiting for me. The organ rang loudly as I walked up the nave, but I hardly noticed the distinguished Cardinal who rose to greet me. Only two faces caught my attention: the lovely and pale face of a girl with a glorious crop of Elphberg hair and a man, whose black hair, red cheeks and dark eyes suggested that this was Black Michael, my 'brother'.

On seeing me, his cheeks grew pale and his helmet crashed to the floor. It was like he could not believe how King Rudolf could be in Strelsau.

I don't remember anything of what happened next, except that the Cardinal anointed me and I accepted the crown of Ruritania and wore it, swearing to keep the oath of the office of the King. A herald's voice cried out, 'Her Royal Highness, Princess Flavia' when the pale-faced lady stepped up and kissed my hand. The Cardinal did the same thing, and handed me a letter from the Pope. The Duke of Strelsau came next, trembling and shaking. I kissed him on both cheeks and we both seemed happy when it was over!

Later, in the carriage, the Princess turned to me and said, 'Rudolf, you look different today.' For me, it was a disturbing remark. I told her that the reception I had been accorded had affected me.

She suddenly said, 'Be careful of Michael…keep a watch on him.'

***

The time was five o'clock. By midnight, I'd be just 'Rudolf Rassendyll' again, I jokingly told Sapt. However, he was in no mood for humour and readied the horse for us to take flight to Zenda. We were soon galloping along the road to our destination, when we heard the sound of horses following us. We stopped and hid by the wayside. Soon, our followers came into our view. They were the Duke and a brawny fellow called Max Holf. Max was Johann's brother and his Highness's servant.

Black Michael asked his companion, 'Which way do we go?'

His companion answered, 'The castle, to find out the truth.'

And they set off towards the castle. A short while later, Sapt and I restarted our journey.

A deathly silence greeted us when we arrived at the lodge. We saw the handkerchiefs Sapt had used to bind the old woman. Inside the lodge, we saw Josef, lay dead on the ground. It was obvious that he had been killed. The King was nowhere to be found. They had kidnapped him and killed his guard!

***

Sapt and I discussed our next plan of action. We held differing views but decided that we must return to Strelsau. A little while later, we heard the sound of hooves. Eight of Black Michael's men were approaching the lodge. They had come to get rid of the evidence of their evil deeds. Sapt and I decided to take them on.

Soon we were battling them. I killed two of the men, and injured one of my fingers when a bullet struck my hand. After the fight ended, we took to the high road, stopping only once—to get my wound treated. Then we took to the road again and soon arrived in Strelsau.

***

In the castle, Sapt extended my lessons on being the King of Ruritania, and I did my best to rule the country. Then, we met Fritz to discuss what do next.

Fritz said, 'Black Michael is back in Strelsau, but only half of his "Six" are with him.'

Sapt exclaimed, 'Then the other three are guarding the King. Which means His Majesty is alive!'

'Who or what is "Michael's Six"?' I asked, confused.

That is when I learnt that these six men—three Ruritanians, the others a Belgian, a Frenchman and an Englishman—were part of Michael's household. He owned them completely, and they would do anything for him, however wrong it may be. They had not been among those we fought at the lodge.

Princess Flavia was the most beautiful woman I had seen and I was well received by her. I struggled to keep her devoted and yet indifferent to me.

We talked of several things, particularly about Michael, his six henchmen, and my relationship with him. She spoke about some court protocol which I was not aware about and I mentally cursed Fritz for not updating me.

I asked Flavia to call for Michael and she said he was sitting in a room nearby. I walked into a side room, where Michael was seated at a table, with a smile on his face. Fritz was fooling around with Princess Flavia's handmaid, Countess Helga. Michael took the hand I held out to him but it soon became clear that he was unhappy that I was with the Princess. When he observed my injured hand, I said that I had hurt myself while playing with a mongrel dog.

Flavia said anxiously, 'Will you not be in danger. Has not the dog been destroyed?'

I replied, 'No. We will wait to see if the dog's bite is harmful.'

Michael asked sourly, 'And if the dog's bite is harmful?'

'Then he will be given a fatal blow to the head, brother,' I said.

He said suddenly, 'I want you to meet three of my most faithful friends who are now in the antechamber.'

And so I met, face-to-face, three of the Six: De Gautet, the tall and lean Ruritanian; Bersonin, the portly and bald Belgian; and Detchard, the Englishman with a narrow face, a bronzed complexion and short, fair hair. These three worthies did not quite conceal their true feelings for me, or I for them!

After making some small talk I left, but not before kissing the fair Flavia's hand.

***

Later, Sapt came rushing into my room. He had confirmed information that the King was being held a prisoner at the castle in Zenda. I also received a letter from Madam de Mauban. She said she had information that would help me. When I met her, Madam de Mauban said that Black Michael had hatched a plan to overthrow the King, and make Princess Flavia his queen. This piece of news caused me much distress.

I later learnt that she was in love with Michael, who had promised to marry her. However, once she found out about his evil plan she decided to help us. She urged me to leave the country at once since half of the Six had set out to murder me. Thanks to her warning, I was ready when the three men attacked, and did not receive a single scratch in the fight. The following afternoon, Sapt came to meet me. He gave me the information that the Duke, three of the Six, and Madam de Mauban had left Strelsau for Zenda.

That night a dance was held at the Palace where I had the opportunity of dancing with Flavia and getting to know her. I confessed my love for her—and she replied that she loved me, too. Not just that; I realized that she loved me—Rudolf Rassendyll—and not 'the King'. I attempted to tell her the whole truth, but Sapt stopped me. The news about our love spread throughout the kingdom and the citizens showed their appreciation for the match, for they loved Flavia—and me, I suppose—very much. They cheered loudly for us.

I was in a dilemma, torn between my love for Flavia and honour for the King. I choose the latter and decided to rescue the King from the Duke's clutches. And so along with Sapt, Fritz and ten other strong and worthy men, I set forth for Zenda. Sapt spread the word that we were going out hunting. Indeed we were hunting—we were hunting a very big boar!

However, I had one more task to perform before I left the Ruritanian capital. I asked for Marshal Strakencz, and when he came to meet me I informed about him my plans. I told him the whole story, and asked him to rule the kingdom in my absence, along with Princess Flavia. If anything happened to the King, she should be crowned Queen of Ruritania, I told him. After briefing the Marshal, we set out to save the King.

***

Black Michael despatched his three Ruritanians to take care of me at the castle. I disguised myself and went with Fritz to the inn in Zenda. There, I told the innkeeper's daughter that I was really the King, and asked her to tell Johann to meet her at the bridge outside Zenda at ten o'clock. Sapt warned me that I must be very careful for great dangers lay ahead.

***

Soon, another of Michael's henchmen, a Ruritanian nobleman called Rupert of Hentzau, brought me an offer from his boss: the Duke would pay me a million crowns if I were to leave Ruritania forever. I turned down this offer and Rupert tried to kill me with a dagger. My left shoulder was wounded and I could not fight back; thus, Rupert made good his escape.

Later, we caught Johann, and he told us where in the castle the King was being held. He also warned me that the King would be in serious danger if we attacked the castle to save the King. So Fritz, Sapt and I put our heads together to chalk out a plan. The three of us were unanimous about one thing: whatever we did, we had to quickly.

***

Meanwhile, Johann reported that the King was sick and that getting worse every passing day. So Fritz, Sapt and I took six men with us, and headed to the castle to rescue his majesty.

'Are you sure the King is still alive?' I asked Sapt when we got there.

'Very probable. Besides the fact that three of Michael's Six are there, the drawbridge is kept up,' Sapt replied, pointing to the drawbridge.

'Besides,' he went on, 'no one goes in without an order from young Rupert or Black Michael himself.'

I searched the moat to see if we could use it as a rescue route. I found Max Holf asleep in a boat in the moat, and killed him just as he woke up.

Lauengram, Kaufstein and Rupert Hentzau caught sight of us and attacked. A furious fight started. Kaufstein and Lauengram and three of my men lost their lives, but Rupert escaped by diving into the moat. Since we were now unable to help the King we returned to the castle of Tarlenheim, which belonged to Count Stanislas von Tarlenheim, a distant relative of Fritz's.

By then, I had problems of my own! The Ruritania Chief of Police told me that the British Ambassador was looking for a missing man—me! So, in desperation, I asked Rupert to come over to my side; but he refused. Instead, he asked me to join him in a plot to kill both the Duke and the King.

***

Soon, the date for the royal wedding was fixed. This meant I had to rescue the King before that date; otherwise, I would end up marrying Princess Flavia! The Duke went into a rage when he heard about the wedding. He kept quarrelling with Madam de Mauban and Rupert of Hentzau, still planned to kill both the Duke and the King, and grab the throne for himself. Besides, the King's health continued to decline; Michael had also jailed the King's doctor. I decided that I would rescue the King the very next morning.

***

Things were coming to a head! I started off alone, leaving Fritz and Sapt behind. At the Castle of Zenda, I was crossing the moat when I saw Rupert in Antoinette's room. She was angry and the two were arguing. Then, the Duke entered the room, and Rupert and De Gautet left the castle. However, a little while later, I spotted Rupert swimming in the moat towards Antoinette's room.

***

The lights went out in the castle. Antoinette screamed when the lights came back; Rupert and the Duke were locked in a hand-to-hand battle. Rupert stabbed Black Michael with his sword. Other servants rushed in, as the blood spurted out onto their master's shirt. We all joined in the fighting. I killed De Gautet, and grabbed the keys to the King's cell. Along the way, I fought Detchard and Bersonin, and left their corpses where they fell. However, Detchard managed to kill the doctor, and I also got wounded in the bargain. The King was in a bad condition, and I thought he was dead. Just then, Sapt and his men entered the castle. Antoinette had really loved Michael and wanted revenge. So she shot at Rupert. He escaped, however, and flung himself out of the window, into the moat. At this point, I found my friends at the scene.

***

In the meantime, Sapt found the King, and finding him barely alive, took him back to Michael's chambers. Antoinette had been praying over the Duke's body. When Sapt entered, she paused from her prayers and cleaned the King's wounds. She then sat with him, while they waited for a doctor. Sapt then sent Fritz to look for me.

Although I was very weak, I gave chase to Rupert and almost killed him after attacking him. In a frenzied fight, Fritz arrived in time to save me and Rupert escaped again.

***

Sapt then put out word that the King had been injured while saving his unnamed friend, and would be resting in private. Thus, the switch had been made again. I was back to being plain old Rudolf Rassendyll. The most important thing was that the King was safe. Princess Flavia heard the rumours and rode to Zenda with the Marshal and his guards. Sapt met them on the way, and told the Princess about my true identity.

The King thanked me for saving his life and, therefore the royal throne. Fritz then beckoned to me to come to another room, where Princess Flavia was waiting for me. We both knew that honour was more important than our love for each other. So we said our goodbyes and I left Ruritania on a happy note. For a while I stayed in the Alps where I took in the cool mountain air. On returning to England, I refused the Sir Jacob's offer to be his attaché in Ruritania. I meet Fritz and his wife once a year and, every year, Queen Flavia and I exchange a bouquet of roses.

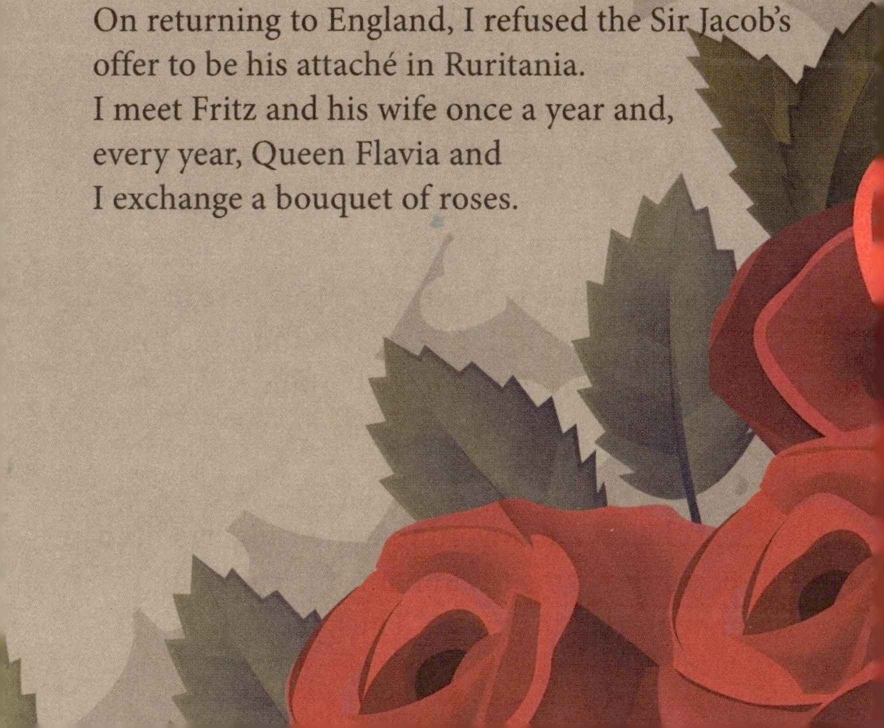

Other Titles *in the* Series

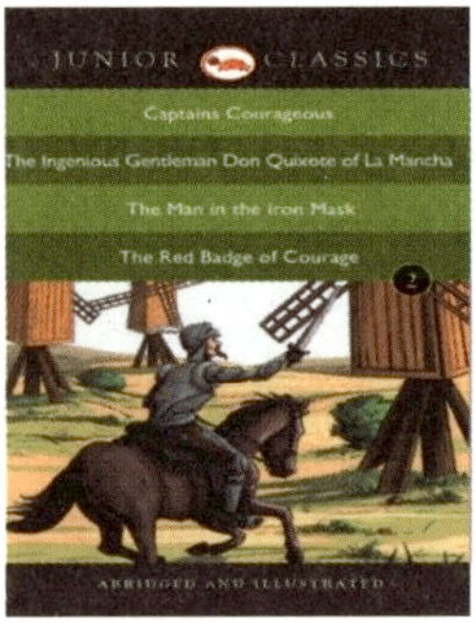

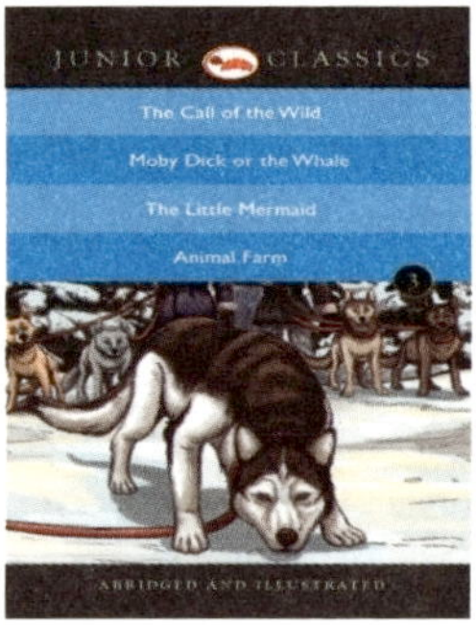

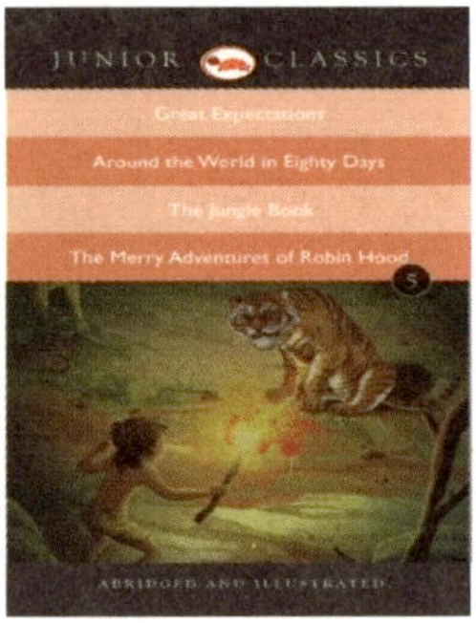

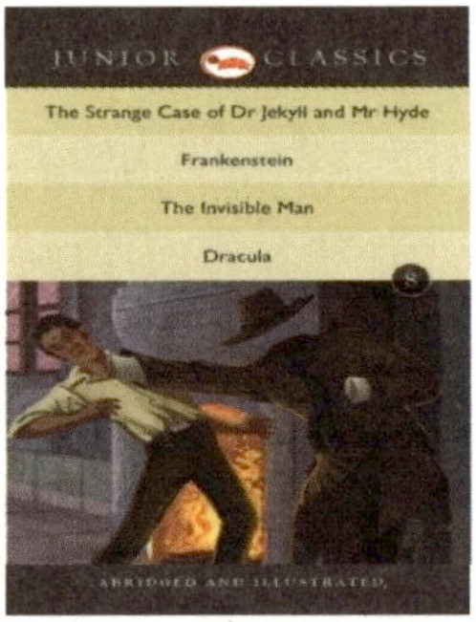